tyler lockhardt

Defense

NEW YORK TIMES BESTSELLING AUTHOR
RAINE MILLER
writing as Brit DeMille
SMOKE
Show

HOME OF THE
VEGAS
CRUSH
TYLER LOCKHARDT
DEFENSE
VEGAS
CRUSH

SMOKE Show

dedication

NUMBER SEVENTY-FIVE

Watching your fights has been my delight.

definition

smoke·show /smōk/·/SHō/
 noun

1. A word to describe someone so hot that you basically see the smoke coming off them...

○ *informal usage*
   (A sexy bombshell walks into a bar.)

Dude 1: *"Dude, check out the smokeshow that just walked in."*

Dude 2: *"Holy f#ck, she really is a smokeshow!"*

1
saint georg

Zoya

January

I say a little prayer to the registration gods that they will not shut me out of the classes I really want.

My draft class schedule in hand, I look down the line, which is so very long I fear I will be standing here forever. Unfortunately, I missed the cutoff for registering online because my overprotective father only just decided that I could follow my sister Irina to UNLV where she is pursuing her master's degree in women's studies. So now, I must stand in the line and pray.

Luckily, most of my transfer credits came through from my previous university in Saint Petersburg, so I am in a slightly better position to get the more targeted classes that I need. It has been my dream to study in the U.S. for a long time even though my father was absolutely against it. With every fiber in his body, he opposed sending me here for college on my own. But now, since my sister got into grad school, he finally agreed. Also helpful is the fact our brother plays professional hockey for the Vegas Crush and makes Las Vegas his home. If not for that perk, I doubt I would even be here at all. Georg is married now, and our father has threatened him with bodily harm if he doesn't look out for me (mostly) but also my sister. This idea would have been laughable a couple of years ago, but now my brother is more settled, less wild, and I believe he has my father convinced that he will keep an eye out for us.

This is not a problem for me.

I do not get in trouble.

My sister, however? Well, let us just say my brother will be having his hands full with Irina. Which is why it is laughable that I had to beg for a year to come here to study in the first place.

I finally make it to the front of the line and work through my class list with the registrar. Two of my classes are already full but she helps me find alternatives that should be suitable. Once everything is in place, I'm shuffled to the bursar's line, where I wait for the privilege of handing over a check for the cost of this semester's tuition.

"Where are you from?" the gray-haired woman at the bursar's desk asks as she enters my payment information into her computer.

"Saint Petersburg." I can anticipate the conversation that will likely follow.

"Florida?"

"Russia."

She looks up and giggles. "Right. The accent should have made it obvious, huh? We just see so many people from so many places here. It's a real melting pot, Las Vegas. Have you noticed that?"

I start to answer, but she keeps talking.

"You speak very good English. I'm really impressed. Have you studied long?"

"Well, my family has always traveled internationally. Everyone in my house speaks both English and Russian fluently."

"Oh, that's really great," the woman chatters. "What made you all travel so much?"

"My father is a youth hockey coach. And my brother plays professionally. He played in the Olympics for the Russian team and now he is here, playing in the NHL."

Her eyes narrow as she peers at the screen, then she looks at me with a surprised look on her face. "Kolochev is your family name?"

"Yes, ma'am."

"Is your brother Georg Kolochev, then?"

"For nineteen long years, unfortunately, yes."

She giggles. "I'm sure all sisters feel that way about their brothers. But yours, my dear, has really made our city proud lately. The Crush are such a great team. They've had a heck of a season so far."

"I guess," I answer with a shrug.

I find hockey talk so boring. Probably because I've spent my entire life in ice-hockey facilities, either watching my father coach or watching my brother and my cousin Boris, play. Boris Drăghici, NHL superstar extraordinaire, was recently traded to Las Vegas from his former team in Austin, Texas, so he is also here playing for the Crush now...but I wisely left that part out. I've dealt with it all my life. The gushing praise from fan girls all over the world enthralled with my hockey-playing male relatives. *So obnoxious.* Honestly, I just want my receipt so I can leave. And by the sound of the dramatic sighing behind me, the others waiting in this line would very much appreciate me to be on my way as well.

When I finally burst through the doors and out into the warm, Vegas sunshine, I'm ready to scream. Thankfully, my sister is waiting for me, two green tea frappuccinos in hand. I gratefully grab one and suck down the icy, sweet concoction with an audible, happy sigh.

"Um, you're welcome?"

"Thank you, Rina." Only I am ever allowed to use the shortened version of her name. "This makes up for the hockey talk I had to endure. Georg this and Georg that. It made me want to erupt like a volcano."

"Don't be so dramatic. Papa wouldn't have let you come here if not for Georg."

"He let me come because of you, too. And how is Georg the responsible one, all of a sudden?"

"Valid point." Irina lifts a shoulder. "He's always been the bad boy and now he is married so he is a saint suddenly."

Saint Georg. What a joke!

My sister and I are both tall and slender. We modeled in Russia when we were kids. My sister tries to cover up her looks by dressing like a punk rocker. Her hair is currently dye-dipped so that her normally dark locks have hot pink ends. She is wearing a black leather jacket over a bright yellow tube top, black combat boots tied below white leggings. This is in comparison to my very boring ensemble of white T-shirt and khaki shorts with Crocs. Normal campus wear if you ask me.

As we walk, we get looks. It happens everywhere we go, and my sister finds it absolutely annoying. Every single time a guy looks at us, she tells him to stop ogling. "Not a piece of meat, asshole," is one of her favorite lines. It makes me turn eight shades of red every time, because I would rather there were simply no confrontations when we walked together.

When two guys stop, asking us first where we got our drinks (as if the logo of the coffeeshop isn't emblazoned on the cups), then if we are angels sent straight from heaven, "That is the lamest thing I've ever heard a dude say," Irina sneers in response.

"They are just giving us compliments." I put my hand on her arm, trying to stop a meltdown.

"Oh, accents!" the shorter of the two says, actually clapping and hopping up and down. He is cute in a generic way, with a snap-back hat and skater-chic T-shirt on.

"Oh, you can go straight to hell! We're not here for

your amusement." Irina digs her heels in for a confrontation. Once again.

"You can't walk around looking like that and expect dudes not to look at you." The other guy— much taller than his friend, with dark hair that flops in his eyes—leers at her bared midriff and ample breasts in the tiny tube top.

"I can walk around *naked* if I want," she snaps. "It wouldn't give you the right to look at me."

"But I *would* look at you, because you'd be naked," tall-guy counters, not giving up so easily.

Hat-guy adds, "Are you two, like, a package deal? Because I think we're down with a group thing, if that's what it takes. Do you kiss each other?"

I cringe at how crass they are but try to pull my sister away from them. Irina has put down roots though, becoming immovable. "You two need your mouths rinsed with bleached. You think you can talk to women that way and get a pass? Do you ever watch the news? It's called rape culture, asshole, and you are perpetuating it!"

At that, the guy in the snap-back has the decency to back off. His hands go up as if he's surrendering. "Hey, we're just playin'—"

His friend, however, tilts his head. His eyes narrow and his mouth curves into what feels like an evil smile. It creeps me out, and the feeling is only made worse when he says, "I'm sure we'll see you both around, babes."

They walk away and I go into a full, involuntary body shudder before dragging my sister—now shouting profanities in Russian—toward the dorms. When she finally stops yelling, the guys are well out of hearing range. She takes a drink of her frap then makes a face. "*Pridurki.* Now my drink is melted."

"Well, we could have avoided that whole argument if you would have ignored them. Why can't you ever ignore *imbetsily* like them?"

"Why do they get to talk to us like that? I didn't give them permission, and there was no good reason for it. I am not going to stand around allowing men to talk to me like I am an object, and you shouldn't either."

"They thought we were hot. We get it all the time. Why does every compliment have to lead to a discussion on rape culture?"

"Asking us if we kiss each other is not a compliment, Zoya," my sister scolds sharply. "Whatever. I just want to be left alone to get my schooling done, and the simple act of walking down the street with you always brings confrontation like that one. *Eto nelepo.*"

"*You* are ridiculous," I snap. "It is not me causing a scene all the time."

"It is not a scene," she argues. "I am putting entitled men in their place. You have heard of #MeToo, haven't you?"

All I can do is roll my eyes. I swear. My sister is like a stone wall when she is like this, and no amount of arguing, begging, or pleading will make her stop ranting. On one hand, I appreciate my sister for being such a committed feminist. On many topics, I agree with her. And no, I do not think some *pridurok* should be able to treat me like a sex toy, but I also don't feel the need to cause a commotion about every single comment that is made, either. Irina, though? She does not let one slip by, ever, and it often ends up embarrassing me.

A lot.

"Don't roll your eyes at me," she says. "You need to woman up and stop letting men gape at you like you're a piece of meat."

"They do not gape at meat the way they gape at us."

"That does not make it better, Zoya. You need to grow a backbone and stop these men from thinking they can demean you with their looks and words and disgusting behaviors. Allowing it makes them think they have permission to do whatever they want."

"I have heard all this before," I say, shaking my head furiously. "Calm down and stop trying to make me into a mini version of you. You can think however you want. I want to go to my classes and make friends like a normal American college student."

As we walk, we keep arguing, finally making our way to my dorm room. Since I am a second-year, I have to stay in the dorms. However, one perk to having a pro-hockey player for a brother is that I was able to get a single room and don't have to share with a roommate. This is best for me, as I am not always a people person. Irina is much more outgoing. Extroverted. Engaging with people often wears me out and I think it will be best, as it was in

Russia, if I have a private space to go to after each day is done.

"This is a nice, little room," Irina says, looking around. "No hockey anything, though? Papa will be so disappointed."

"*Bez raznitsy.*" I shrug. "He is not here."

Irina is smirking, so I know she is joking. She hates hockey marginally less than I do, as she hates their drinking and womanizing. She and our brother, Georg, have had many arguments over the years, since he was always a poster boy for both of those vices. Not so much these days, of course. He is now sober and found the love of his life in his new wife, Pam. They are both very good for each other. Our parents love her, probably mostly because the timing of her entry into my brother's life coincided with him having the best playing year of his life, and consequently the best contract he has ever had, as well. In my parents' eyes, Pam is a miracle worker. And their marriage was a miracle worker for me, too. If my brother wasn't sober and married, my father never would have let me come here for the rest of my schooling. Irina is living off campus in an apartment with two other roommates, which I would prefer if I had any say in my situation. One of the conditions of our deal was that I had to live on campus for the first year. Papa doesn't approve of Irina's choices most of the time, so it was accept this condition or not come to Vegas at all.

I flop on my bed and wave to my sister as she heads for the door. "See you later, Rina."

"Having a famous brother can have its perks," she answers, looking around my room one more time. "I had the smallest room in undergrad with two roommates who smelled like fish."

She leaves and I am left thanking the hockey gods that I do not have any roommates. Especially not ones who smell like fish.

2
no finesse at all

Tyler

I stick my glasses on my face and wipe the steam off the mirror, rubbing my five-o'clock shadow and trying to decide if I should shave or not. I just got in a killer workout, followed by a hot shower. The locker rooms are oddly quiet, creepy even, without the noise of a bunch of dudes.

I'm glad the holiday break is over. It's been too damn long with everyone out of town and I'm ready to be back on the ice. We're having a banging season, so this year, I've set my sights on my name finally gettin' carved into Lord Stanley's motherfucking Cup. Everybody should have some life goals. It's my year, I can feel it. Of course, Vegas has to pull off another championship season for it to happen.

I decide against the shave—chicks dig the shadow —but acknowledge I need to stop at the barber shop for a trim to my undercut. Gettin' a little shaggy and can't have the flow lookin' raggedy as we hit the ice in the new year. I head to my locker to dress just as a text comes through.

Viktor: I cannot meet you for drinks as planned.

Tyler: The fuck?

Viktor: We are all jetlagged.

Tyler: Get over it. Be a big boy.

Viktor: It is different with a baby and a wife.

Tyler: So Red doesn't want you out tonight?

Viktor: She is fine with it. I am just tired.

Tyler: Not much of a wingman these days. Disappointing.

Viktor: Do not be such a baby, man.

Tyler: Go change your baby's diaper or something.

Viktor: Change your own diaper.

I send him a GIF of a guy giving the middle finger, then follow with a winky-face emoji so he knows I'm not really all that mad. I mean, yeah, it's a wicked pisser that my big-ass best friend is now tied down to a lady-love and tiny baby person, but I also get it.

Scarlett's hot as hell. If I found a piece like that, I might...

Babies? Nah. Not so much. I'm not sure Viktor would've chosen to have a baby so fast, either, but whoops. Now he's got one, and boy, has it fucked up our social life. Curses to babies and relationships. I'm staying single until the day I die. No one needs that ball and chain. No way.

What I do need? A stiff drink and a hockey honey on my lap. I send out a couple of texts and my buddy, Terrence, who works in ticketing, shoots back that he's already out and I should get my ass out there with him. Done. Don't have to tell me twice.

I make the three-block walk down to a club, finding Terrence and two other guys from sales already half-drunk and surrounded by women. The more the merrier, I always say. I sit my ass down and order everyone a round.

"Good man!" Terrence salutes me, his arm muscles bulging to the delight of the women sitting near him. They fawn all over him like he's Idris Elba or something.

"Hey, *I'm* the pro, here," I say, making a muscle and winking at the girls, "so give this guy some love, too."

"You kidding?" Terrence asks, his grin wide. "They only came because I said my man Locksey is on the team."

"That's better," I say as one of the girls crawls onto my lap. Terrence and I clink beer bottles and I swig some back. "I've gotta use whatever I can, man, 'specially when my friends are as good-lookin' as this motherfucker."

Terrence rolls his eyes, but that dude knows he's good-lookin'. I swear to God, the Crush only hires good-looking people. I can't think of a single person who works for the place who isn't at least semi-attractive. And I'm under no illusions that I'm even close to the top of the hotness list. Fuck, I mean even my big, dumb friend Viktor looks like he was molded out of clay.

No, I'm just a poor kid from South Boston with a bad attitude, a hot temper, and a marginally good defensive spirit. I got lucky somehow, got a smidge of talent, and a lot of grit. And so-so looks, I suppose. Coulda done worse.

"Where's the big man tonight?" Terrence asks after we drain our beers and order another round.

"Bah," I grunt, waving a hand like I swatting away a fly. "Just got back from Mother Russia. Everyone's jetlagged, according to him. I think he's just being a big puss."

Terrence raises a shoulder. "Meh. I mean, his old lady probably doesn't want him out in places like this anymore, especially now that they've got a baby."

"Are you talking about Viktor Demoskev?" the girl on my lap asks.

"Yes, ma'am. Giant Russian bastard and my best friend."

"You two play so well together out there," she says, fawning.

"We aim to please, doll."

Terrence leans forward, grinning. "I need them to play well so I can sell a shit-ton of ticket packages. You know, there was a time when we couldn't sell half of the seats in that arena. Once Kolochev got dry, you two peckers gelled on D, and the Ice Dragon got set up at center, we were on fire. The coaching staff's gotta be nutting themselves over such a lineup."

"I think it's you who's nutting himself 'cause of all that bank you're makin' on commission. Plus, I know you think I'm damn pretty." I grin at him and wink at the girl.

We have a couple more rounds before the place starts to liven up for the night, a DJ coming on to spin some EDM. The girls have staked their claim, evil-eyeing any other woman who tries to approach. It's kind of a shame, really, since these girls are just...okay. Not hard on the eyes or anything, just not knockouts. Actually, they're fine to look at, and at the end of the day, beer goggles are a guy's best friend. It's not like they'll get anything more than a one-night stand anyway.

They're jabbering about what they do for a living. One's a teacher or some shit, and she keeps talking about how teaching has pretty much made her positive she never wants kids. That's encouraging, I suppose. I only tune in and out to be polite. I don't really care what any of them has to say. I don't need to know their favorite color or where they grew up. I'm not interested in whether or not they have pets. But I do need to pretend to be listening, at least, and so I watch the crowd and tune in every so often just to nod in agreement or answer a direct question.

The most recent is, "Do you want to dance?"

"Yep," I say, standing and giving a big stretch. The woman who was on my lap earlier is blonde with big tits. She's the teacher who doesn't want any kids. I take her hand and haul her out to the dance floor, where we grind on each other as the crowd thickens around us. She's a decent dancer, I'll give her that. She turns around and bends up and down, her ass on full display in a skin-tight, stretchy dress. I bet her employer would have something to say about this kind of behavior.

Before long, we're lined up against each other, one of my legs between hers, rubbing at that most sensitive place. She's got her hands on my ass and I'm semi-hard.

"You want to go somewhere for a fuck?" she asks against my ear.

Bingo.

I nod and we push back through the crowd and up to the quieter second floor. We find a mostly unoccupied women's room and barge into a stall, kissing as we struggle to make room in a tiny space for two people—one of them a six-foot-two hockey player.

I push her dress up to her waist and shove a hand inside her barely-there panties. She's soaking wet. Totally ready. She moans as I finger fuck her, two fingers in and out. I'm being careless, not using any kind of finesse, but she still seems to like it. In fact, I know she likes it because she breaks out in a high-pitched whine and then her pussy clenches around my fingers as she comes all over them.

"My turn." I pull my cock from my jeans and she ogles it, making some nonsense about how big it is.

There really isn't room to fuck in here, and frankly, I'm not sure I want to. I press lightly on her shoulders and she takes the hint, making her way to her knees, her dress still up around her waist. She takes my balls in one hand and wraps the other hand around the base of my cock as she slurps my cock like a popsicle. She licks along the length, then swirls her tongue around the head. It's good. Feels good, but I want her mouth around my cock. I want the tip to touch the back of her throat, so I encourage her to open up for me. She does, but I can tell she's not into giving me a good deep-throat, so I don't fuck her mouth like I planned. Instead, I let her do her thing, and it takes a few minutes but with some concentration, I'm able to get off. She swallows, grimacing, and I know that'll be the end of the action between the two of us tonight. She can't take me balls-deep and she acts like swallowing jizz is the worst thing ever. It's time to say thank you and goodnight now.

I help her back up, straightening her dress and stuffing myself back into my pants before we step out of the tiny stall. I wash my hands as she splashes water from the sink in her mouth, swirling it around and spitting it out. She's still at the mouth-rinsing as I head out. When I get back to the table, Terrence is grinning.

"How was it, champ?" he asks.

"Lackluster. Think I'm gonna go." And sadly, that's all it's been lately. Yeah, it's sex. Relieves some pressure. But what's the point of a hot mouth or pussy that I have to work to enjoy? *Defeats the purpose, doesn't it?*

He raises a shoulder. "Suit yourself."

"See ya later." I wave and make for the door.

Fifteen minutes later, I'm on my couch in nothing but boxers, playing Fortnite on the PS4. Username IceDragon90 is online, so I grab my headphones and invite him to chat.

"Hey, asshole, back from Nerd Town, are we?"

"If, by Nerd Town, you mean the most magical place on earth, then yes," Boris's girlfriend, Talia, responds. "Boris is grabbing a drink from the fridge."

"Hey, if it isn't the hot librarian," I tease.

"I'm not a librarian, Tyler. Investment manager, remember?"

I hear some muffled talking, then Boris comes over the headset. "And she's making me a killing already."

"Guess I need to make an appointment," I say. "My investments are all over the place."

"I thought you were going to say your investments are drowning in beer," Boris taunts.

"Hardy har har. I'll have you know I'm wicked

good at budgeting. I have a beer budget that I strictly adhere to."

"To which I strictly adhere," Talia interjects.

"Grammar police much? Jesus. Go learn a book, darlin'. Let the big boys play."

"Let the big boys play a game for children?" she asks.

I have no answer for that, so I just snort. This is the way things are with Talia, who I thought was a shrinking violet, nerd-type but is really sassy and smart and not afraid to cuss or swear or say whatever damn thing pops into her Brainiac head. She's a good match for Boris, who is way more reserved. He comes out of his shell for her.

I'd never admit this to anyone, but honestly? All the guys have found women who make them better. They all seem happier and more secure now that they're in relationships. It's cool I guess. Doesn't mean I want to be within smelling radius of a relationship myself, but good for anyone who finds something meaningful.

While Boris and I play a round, he and Talia tell me about their recent trip to Harry Potter World in Orlando, where Talia got to pick out a wand and wear a cape or some other nerdy shit. She seems way excited about all of it, though I have no idea what the hell she's talking about.

It's pretty late when I hear some smoochy sounds that lead to whispering and giggling. I could take a bet on how long before—

"Hey, I'm out. Got to get my princess to bed."

"Gotta get laid, is more like," I mumble, rolling my eyes as IceDragon90 logs off.

And now I'm alone in my apartment, playing a children's video game—alone—wide awake and wishing all my friends weren't tied to the ball-n-chain of their dreams.

3
not talking hockey

Zoya

Two weeks later.

My biology professor is a tiny, gray-haired woman with a voice that could put a person to sleep. She just drones on and on, barely taking a breath, and certainly not inviting questions or discussion about the topic at hand.

Honestly, I am not a math or science person by nature, so this would be boring even if someone really amazing was teaching. I front-loaded the last of the tier 1 math and science I needed into this semester in hopes I could get it all out of the way and then focus on the fun stuff next semester. Now I am almost regretting it, but *c'est la vie*.

In order to get through what I am sure could be classified as cruel and unusual punishment; I doodle. It's just a loose portrait rendering of my mom, who I miss more than I expected since being in the States.

The guy sitting next to me leans over and whispers, "That's really good."

I turn and catch his eye. "Thanks. Just doodling."

He's cute, this guy, with wavy, long-ish hair that curls around the collar of his blue polo shirt. The way he grins at me makes me blush and shut my notebook, straightening up and trying to pay better attention to the class.

He pokes my notebook with his finger. "Why are you embarrassed?"

"I am not," I say. "I should be paying better attention."

"This woman is a fossil," he whispers. "She must be a hundred years old and I swear she hasn't taken one breath the entire lecture."

I can't help but giggle. "That is what I was just thinking."

"See? Great minds think alike. We should be friends."

Thankfully, class ends and I'm able to divert from the conversation as I gather my things. Still, the guy follows close on my heels. Outside, he catches up and says, "I'm Jay, by the way."

"Zoya." We shake hands, which I suppose is better than him ogling my breasts or something. And he is shorter than me, which is kind of a funny surprise. By at least two inches.

"Wow," he says. "You're taller when you're standing up."

Chuckling, I say, "I only stopped growing last year. My father and sister are tall, also."

"Are your sister and father also Russian?"

One side of my mouth quirks up. "Who says I am Russian?"

"Okay. Are your sister and father also supermodels?"

"Nope, we are all just tall people with very strange accents. And yes, we are from Russia. And no, my father would never let me model past the age of ten, unless maybe for turtlenecks."

He shrugs. "I think you'd look pretty good in a turtleneck. Or a plastic bag. Or really anything, honestly. But your dad is strict, I take it."

I nod. "Very. It took a lot of work to get him to agree to let me come to Las Vegas for school. And only because my sister came to do her master's in Vegas and my older brother lives here that he even considered it."

"Well," he says, folding his arms and appraising me, "I'm very curious to hear more, but I also have a huge need for caffeine. I think our teacher might be an energy vampire. Can I help renew your energy level as well?"

"I cannot. I have to get back to change for a post-holiday party with the Crush."

Jay's eyes widen. "Whoa. I'm impressed. How did you score that invite?"

"My brother plays for them."

"Who's your brother?"

"Georg Kolochev. On defense."

He laughs out loud like I've said the funniest

thing. "He's not just on defense. Seriously? Your brother is Curious Georg?"

I roll my eyes and let out an epic sigh. "Here we go again."

"What's that mean?"

"It means I am tired of everyone going fanboy over my brother. Hockey is not that important in the grand scheme of life."

"Uh, I beg to differ. Especially here. People are apeshit over the Crush, and every one of those first-string players...they're like gods. You should be proud of your brother. He's a superstar."

"He is just my goofy brother. And I grew up around hockey, so I was really hoping to come here and not have to see hockey or talk hockey or think about hockey every minute."

"Wrong town, wrong time, Zoya." He shakes his head at me. "Las Vegas loves the Crush and they love hockey. And it's about to get worse if they keep playing like total studs and win the Cup again."

"Great. Well, then I regret to inform you that I will not be able to be friends with you, Jay from biology class. I simply cannot be friends with a person who obsesses over hockey. It is my personal principle for which I make no exceptions."

"Well, I'm sorry to hear that. If I promise to never talk hockey in front of you, then can you be my friend?"

I give him an amused grin. "I will consider it."

"I even promise not to geek out if your brother comes around."

"Do not make promises you cannot keep."

"Is that a yes?"

"It is a maybe," I say. "I have to go, but I will see you in class."

AFTER A QUICK SHOWER I throw on a pair of distressed jeans and a sheer, black, sleeveless tunic. I'm working on my hair and makeup when Irina comes through the bathroom door.

"Ever hear of knocking?" I scowl at her through the mirror.

"As if you have any parts I haven't seen before, sister," she retorts.

"What if I had been in here with a man?"

"That is very unlikely."

She is right, but I don't want to admit it. Instead, I take in her outfit—ripped mom jeans and a Pussy Riot T-shirt with Doc Martens.

"That is not at all appropriate for this event." I roll my eyes at her outfit.

"*Yebat' sebya*," my sister hisses.

"So hostile all the time," I say, refocusing on my reflection in the mirror. My hair is long and tousled, still sun-streaked from summer. I opt for simple makeup—nude lip gloss and a little mascara and eyeliner.

"You should wear these with that outfit," Irina says, holding up a pair of red heels. The first helpful thing she has said to me.

I grab the shoes and pull them on, then take in the full look. It feels sexy but edgy, and still appropriate. None of my body parts are on display, so my brother is unlikely to turn eight shades of red and tell me to cover up.

Satisfied that at least one of the two Kolochev sisters looks appropriate for a pro-hockey event, I shoo my sister out the door, locking up before we head out to see our brother for the first time since we all returned to the United States.

4
hands off the sestry

Tyler

Stupid team events. Stupid monkey suit. I hate it. I hate getting all dressed up and acting like a church boy just for the stupid press. Fuckin' annoying. It's not like they haven't heard eight ways to Sunday what we think of the lineup and how happy we are with the season and blah, blah, blah. It makes my head hurt.

Thank God, at least there's a bar at this thing. I head over and get a beer, wishing for something stronger, then beeline for my man Viktor, who stands a head taller than all the other bodies in the room.

"Good to see you, jerkface." I lean in for a bro-hug. "Can't hang with your best friend these days? Too good for your old pal Tyler?"

"Do not be a baby," Viktor growls. "I already have one baby to care for."

"Do not be a Russian robot." I mock his accent —*badly*. "I'm just fuckin' with ya. How's dad life?"

He gives a big yawn, which I pretty much figure is his answer. But then he surprises me.

"I very much enjoy being a father. He is smart already. I can tell he is thinking."

"Babies aren't that smart. Hate to tell you that."

"No, that is not true." He pouts. "Our son is old soul."

"Yeah? An old soul who shits in his pants?"

"He does do that," Viktor agrees. "Very often."

I scratch my chin, wondering if I'm breaking out in hives as the baby talk just goes on and on. And on. Seriously? I think Viktor might be fucking with me, just to make me comatose or something. I have to hear about the time the baby pissed on him during a diaper change, and about the sticky poop he had the other day. It's a goddamn nightmare.

"You know, just fucking shoot me if I ever spend this much time worrying about someone else's shit."

"Is part of being a parent," he says.

"Is making you more boring than usual, which is saying a lot." I mock his accent again just to be a dick.

"You will find someone some day and you will want to be a father," he says. "Mark my words." *Oh fuck no. Not a chance.*

"Eat your words, is more like." I shake my head at him. "You talkin' about poop and puke and whatever other bodily secretions babies make is not a ringing endorsement for the virtues of parenthood, friend. In fact, it's so fuckin' boring that I literally want to go jump in front of the Zamboni just to escape this torture."

"You cannot be a manwhore forever," Viktor argues.

"I sure as shit can. I'm gonna take Viagra and be a baller till the day I die. It's gonna be great in a Hugh Hefner kinda way."

"I hope it works out for you," Viktor says with a smirk. *I do too.* That means I'll have several blondes with enormous tits hanging off me at once without needing to know their names.

Doesn't get better than—holy fuck. *Who the hell is Kolochev and his wife talking to?*

They've got to be sisters, with perfect, supermodel faces. High cheekbones, pouty lips, long, brown hair. Tall. Legs for days. Holy public erection, Batman! One looks like she'd probably bite my nut sack off. She's in a Pussy Riot tee, ripped jeans, and combat boots. Her eyeliner is totally goth and she's got the tips of her long hair dyed bright pink. The don't-fuck-with-me glare is totally working for her. Total turn-on. She probably has hairy pits and a terrible attitude, but she sure is workin' it. Yum. Come to papa.

The other smokeshow looks younger. And a lot more demure. Her brown eyes are wide, and her lips are full and luscious. Ugh. I have to adjust myself because they really are turning me on.

I rib my friend. "Who are those two?"

Viktor laughs at me. Laughs, can you believe it? "They are hands-off."

"Why?" I ask, totally confused. "Why hands-off?"

"They are Kolochev's *sestry*."

"Kolochev's what? I don't speak Russian, bro."

"Sisters," he spits out. "His sisters."

"And what? They're off limits, why?"

"Are you kidding?" Viktor stares me down. "Georg would never let you touch them. He is being protective as their father is protective."

I make a snorting noise of disapproval. "Well, I'm gonna get right past that chastity belt, come hell or high water. Those two are invited on my welcome wagon any time."

Yep, come hell or high water, I'm getting one—or preferably both—of those smokeshows into the sack.

I think I just found my life's mission.

5
i am leaving

Zoya

I roll my neck and blow out a big breath. Enough of the hockey talk already. I have had enough of telling each person I have met tonight that I may major in education or art or some combination of the two. More than enough of the smiling and laughing while people tell me again and again what a wild man my brother was up until recently. It is the same, always, and I just want to go back to my room to study.

"What's wrong?" Georg asks as Irina gets into a conversation with Pam about sexual harassment in the workplace.

I have to roll my eyes. "She never stops."

"Irina?" he asks, glancing at my sister with her crazy-ass outfit and hair before shrugging. "She has always been loud about the things she cares about."

I just shrug back at him.

"Thanks for coming tonight," he says. "It means a

lot. The guys were all excited to hear that you were coming to school here."

"Yes, I have heard that many times tonight," I say before lowering my voice to quote all the dumb things people have said tonight. "*Here to keep your brother in line? What a wild man that guy was. Well, it's a good thing you are here to keep him out of trouble.*"

"Sorry," Georg says, reaching out to pull me into a side hug.

"It is okay," I reassure him. "I knew you had a reputation. The one reason Papa would not let us come over sooner. Only it is just that I—"

"You didn't realize how it would define me here?" I hear sadness in his voice, and see regret on his face.

"I mean, I know you have a good heart. There is more to you than those things, yet those things are all people talk about."

"Well, those things are not who I am anymore," he says, his arm still around my shoulders. "At least, mostly."

I glance to look at him and see the impish smirk that I have known all my life. The glimmer of mischief in his eyes. One thing that has never changed about my brother is his sense of humor. He is a practical joker and a clown. In great contrast to me and my sister. She is more intense. I am more reserved. Sometimes I wonder how the three of us could have come from the same set of parents.

"Well, I am glad you found Pam," I tell him. "Mama is, as well."

"Ah, yes, let the grandchild lobbying effort commence." He grins, shaking his head.

"Well, I would be happy to talk about grandchildren if it meant not talking about you. Georg Kolochev, the superstar hockey player. Hockey this. Hockey that. Can we please talk more about Georg because he is the bright star around which we all revolve?"

Georg pulls his arm from my shoulders and put his hand over his heart, looking wounded. "Ouch, *mladshaya sestra*. That is just mean."

"Sorry, *starshiy brat*," I apologize, feeling a little guilty. Not too much, but a little. "I am just tired. Ready to go home to study. Tired of talking about hockey. May I please be excused, sir?"

He chuckles. "I hardly see you and all you want to do is run away."

"I am happy to see you anywhere other than at a place connected to your livelihood," I offer, giving him a short, fake smile. "I would be happy to spend time with you and Pam at your new condo, and learn more about my sister-in-law.

"I understand," he says, reaching out to tousle my hair like he did when we were children. Then he raises an eyebrow and gives a silly grin. "You know I'm supposed to remind you at least once daily that Papa says you and Irina are to stay away from wild hockey players."

Irina, who has just wandered over to rejoin the conversation, snorts. "I can handle myself and my own body, thank you very much. This is the exact problem with the patriarchy. Women are never allowed to choose for themselves."

Georg and I give the same exact sigh at the same exact time. I cannot know what he is thinking, not exactly—I mean, he married a very feisty, very opinionated, very independent woman. I know my brother is not old-fashioned about gender roles or anything. And neither am I, for that matter. I mostly agree with everything Irina says. I just cannot always agree with how she says it. Often, it is presented as a jab, meant to make everyone around her uncomfortable. It is less of a conversation and more of an abuse. And here, around Georg's teammates and the Crush staff? Is not the place for it.

"My love?" Georg asks Pam in a syrupy-sweet voice. "Would you mind driving the girls back for me? Zoya needs to study."

"Sure," Pam says. "Are you ready to go now? The car is just in the garage."

I start to open my mouth to affirm that I am very much ready to leave, when a tall, broad-shouldered, blond guy steps into our paths. He holds out a hand and meets my gaze, a cocky grin on his face.

"I'm Tyler Lockhardt."

I shake his hand, but say, "I am leaving."

He laughs. "That's an interesting name. Doesn't sound Russian, though."

As his suit jacket pulls up, I notice part of a tattoo. Irina steps forward and shakes his hand, too. "That's Zoya, which is Russian for *I have to study*. And I am Irina, which is Russian for *I love your tattoo*."

Tyler grins, a wicked, bad-boy thing that makes my stomach flip-flop. He is trouble with a capital T, I can already tell. My sister will chew him up and spit him out. They will have good times together.

He points at her and winks. "That's good. Real good." He has a slight accent, though I do not know enough about different accents in English to know where it comes from.

"I have been thinking about getting a tattoo," Irina says, eager to keep his attention. My sister has gone from stone-cold patriarchy smasher to dark predator now. Part of my sister's view on feminism is wrapped up in sexual freedom, so...you get the point.

"Is that so?" he asks, cocking his head, seeming genuinely intrigued. "By the looks of you, I'd have guessed you already had one. Or several."

My sister gives him a wolf's grin. "Maybe you can help me with the artistic inspiration."

He smiles right back, all teeth, then leans in and whispers, "Maybe I can. I'd enjoy helping you pop that cherry."

I was not supposed to hear that. I would have preferred not to have heard it. They are both laying it on thick. No doubt, he will be her first Vegas conquest. Well, she can have him. He is a hockey player and I have zero interest in hockey players.

"When did you get your first tattoo?" Irina is asking.

"I gave it to myself," he says with a laugh. "I was fifteen, living in Southie. I used a safety pin, and some of my ma's liquid eyeliner and gave myself a shitty-lookin' baseball on my ankle."

"A baseball?" I ask, unable to control my curiosity.

"Yeah, I mean, every kid in South Boston thinks he's gonna play for the Red Sox at one point. I got it fixed by a professional later who turned it into a hockey puck. No embarrassing evidence to show you, sorry, ladies."

"So that is where your accent is from?" I ask. "From South Boston?"

"Born and raised," he says with a shrug. To Irina, he asks, "How come you haven't gotten one yet?"

"My father is a bit overprotective," she explains.

"True story," I add.

"You don't strike me as a woman who lets men—fathers or otherwise—get in the way of what she wants." Tyler's eyebrows go up, a challenge.

This will probably be it for Irina. If she was not already planning on sleeping with this guy, she certainly is now. They keep talking and I zone out, truly wanting to leave. Still, even though I keep silent and never say another word, Tyler still focuses his gaze on me. Not the whole time—no, he splits his attention between the two of us. When his stare is focused on me, it makes my body go warm. It makes me have a strange feeling; a feeling that makes me feel uncomfortable but also a little excited. The second part makes me angry. I should not think American hockey boys are cute or sexy. We have plenty of handsome men in Russia, and yet... he is cute in a very different way to the other men here. *Rough.*

Less...pretty. His nose is crooked, like it was broken at one point—not uncommon in hockey players.

His skin is tanned from the Las Vegas sun and his eyes are a steely blue-gray. His hair is very blond on the top, darker blond on the bottom, cut short on the sides and in the back, longer on top. He has it styled in a loopy pompadour right now, but I would bet it stays flat and falls in his eyes most of the time. He does not strike me as a fancy guy who does his hair every day.

Not that I am putting that much time into thoughts of this random hockey player. No.

"Lockhardt," Georg finally interjects, back from whatever side conversation he was having. "Get the hell away from my sisters."

"Oh, these are *your* sisters?" Tyler asks innocently, standing to full height and putting a hand over his heart. "I had no idea."

"I think you knew exactly who they were, and I'll tell you now that you will not even look at them from here on out. Not one look. Got it?"

Tyler gives a smug grin. "You're the boss."

Georg lectures him anyway. "My father gave strict instructions to keep these two behind the fence, away from the wild animals. That includes you. Go find someone else to fornicate with."

"Oh my God!" Irina laughs at him. "You sound like an old man."

Even I giggle at our brother's outburst. This is a man who, if the Internet is to be relied on, has probably slept with a good portion of the women in

Vegas. Happily married now, of course, but he was no altar boy before meeting Pam. And now he sounds like someone's grandfather, yelling at people to get off his lawn.

Boy, how times (and brothers) can change. Pam and I make eye contact, and we both burst out laughing. *My poor brother. An old man at thirty years.*

6
almost three-quarters

Tyler

The Feminazi sister definitely wants me. She's gushing over the tattoo on my wrist. Imagine how much she'd cream if she saw everything I've got inked on my body. Plus, if Daddy says no, I'll bet she's just the type to do exactly the opposite. She's an easy mark, for sure.

However, I'm in the mood for a challenge tonight. The younger sister is paying me about a half-percent of attention, which is annoying, but also makes me want to get the other ninety-nine-point-five. Gotta work for it. That's cool with me. I'm feeling her as the quiet one, the soft one who just wants to go put her fuzzy pajamas on and read a book. I wonder if she wears glasses? I wear glasses when I don't have my contacts in. Maybe it would help if she saw me with them on.

As I watch her, it's clear this is really the last place on earth she wants to be. I don't think it's personal toward me—I just think she hates functions like this. *That makes two of us, Smokeshow.*

I turn to her. "You look miserable. Can I create a distraction to help you escape?"

She lights up—literally her whole face lights up—and she looks so relieved. "God, yes. I just want to get back to campus. I have so much work to do for my classes."

"Come on, I'll walk you out to grab a cab."

"Oh, no, I—"

"I don't bite." *Much.*

"It is not that," she says, blushing. "Pam has offered to take us back."

"Ahh. Well, then, tell me about what you're studying." And there is the face I've seen a few times in the past five minutes. *Boredom.* She must've been asked this a million times tonight. Idiot. I'm an idiot.

"Art and education, I think," she answers, though I can tell she's only being polite.

"What will you do after? What's your dream job?"

"Oh, I am not sure. I have always liked little children. I think I might enjoy being a preschool teacher, but I also draw and doodle occasionally, so maybe I could teach art."

Okay, okay, she's livening up. That's progress. She must be young, though, if she's just starting to think about her college major. "How old are you, if you don't mind me asking?" *Please be at least eighteen.*

"Nineteen and almost three-quarters," she says, all soft-spoken and gentle. She looks like a million bucks...a friggin' goddess, but technically still a teenage girl. Damn. That's pretty young. But it's over eighteen, so we're golden. Game on. I snort, thinking of Kolochev's demand. *"My father gave strict instructions to keep these two behind the fence, away from the wild animals. That includes you. Go find someone else to fornicate with."* Oh no, my Russian friend. Quite happy with these beauties.

"The almost three-quarters is wicked important, hey?" I give her a smile that could drop panties down the street in the club I was at the other night with Terrence.

She returns the barest hint of a smile and shrugs. *Smokeshow is a tough crowd.*

"I'm twenty-two," the sister pipes in. "You?"

"I'm pushin' twenty-five. And you two are making me feel like an old, old man."

This makes the older sister laugh, but the younger one looks at Pam as if telegraphing her extreme need to blow this taco stand.

"I'm studying women and gender studies at UNLV," the older sister is saying. "Getting my master's degree now, then I'll go on to get my PhD."

She keeps talking, as a couple of others have joined the group. I tune out, honestly, because school was just a means to an end for me. I got my hockey career out of it, and made it work, but this conversation is not holding me. I focus on the younger sister's hair. The way it flows down her back in sexy, sun-kissed waves. The way it would feel in my hands. God, what was her name? There's never any need to bother remembering names, but I should commit Kolochev's sisters' names to memory. I can't call them *buddy* or Kolochev. I *should* make an effort.

"So," I say quietly to the younger one, "what are your names again? I think I've taken too many head shots. Bad memory lately."

She squints at me in a way that says she sees right through my bullshit. "Zoya. My sister is Irina. I am sure you will not remember in a moment, Tyler Lockhardt. See, I was barely paying attention to you, but I still remembered your name."

So Smokeshow's got sass under that gentle exterior. I like it. I like it a lot. Also? Zoya is a hot name. Flaming hot. Every bit of this chick is hot, including her total ambivalence toward me. Just makes me want her even more. I'll wear her down, just wait. I am a charming and persistent motherfucker.

I start to come up with something witty to say in response, but Georg's wife, Pam, squeals in a way that gives me a sense of how dogs feel when a dog whistle blows. She screams something about Viktor and Scarlett's baby and goes running across the room like a woman possessed, her arms straight out in front of her. She literally grabs the baby from Scarlett's arms, cooing and nearly in tears from whatever delirium takes over a woman when a baby is nearby.

"Christ," Georg says in a horrified whisper. "What in the seventh realm of hell was that all about?"

"Baby fever, brother," I answer.

"No way. Pam and I have talked about this a thousand times. We are both committed to a baby-free existence. She just likes holding the babies, and then *she likes to give them back.* No changing poopy diapers. No having milk come out of her tits. She doesn't want any of that."

"Sounds like maybe *you* just don't want any of that. And I get it."

"No, it is mutual," Georg insists, speaking a bit louder. "We haven't decided if we want to have children ever. I would be a terrible role model. Why expose an innocent to my level of immaturity and dysfunction?"

Irina snorts, picking up on our conversation. "I agree wholeheartedly."

"I do not," Zoya says, her voice soft but assured. "I think you and Pam would be great parents."

"On what grounds?" Georg asks with an incredulous laugh.

"You are very different than you were even a year ago," Zoya says. "You are not drinking. You are stronger on the ice. You have an amazing, smart, educated wife. You both work hard, and you are both committed and loving to each other. You are even helping your sisters further their education. What about any of this seems like it would make you bad parents? It seems like a good home environment for any child, in my opinion."

Georg's mouth hangs open. He snaps it shut and rubs the stubble on his chin. I think he might be emotional, the way he looks away toward nothing. Then he shakes his head. "No way. That's baloney. I'd spawn some sort of holy terror. Or I'd do something dumb to get the kid hurt or—"

"Oh, I see what this is..." Irina interrupts before launching into some psychoanalytical something about Georg and all the reasons he thinks he'd be a shitty dad. Zoya is only half listening—I expect she's heard all this before—craning her neck to find Pam. I think. *Here's my opportunity.*

"Hey, looks like you're ready to head out. I could walk you back to campus if you'd like?"

She looks over at her brother and sister, now engaged in a heated conversation. Pam is still off gushing over the baby. Zoya bites her lip, hesitates, frowns. I can see the wheels turning as she mulls over my offer. Smokeshow is wavering.

"Yes, okay. I need to get back. Thank you."

Boom. I'm in.

7
get a life

Zoya

When we walk out into the night, it is crisp and cool, much cooler than it was when my sister and I left campus. I shiver in my thin tunic top, rubbing my arms for warmth. This hockey player, Tyler, shrugs off his suit jacket and hands it to me.

I gratefully accept, wrapping it around my shoulders. The jacket is huge on me, of course, as he is well over six feet with broad, muscular shoulders. Yes, I noticed this about him. Guilty.

"Thank you. I think I will just call a ride service after all. It is maybe too cool to walk the two miles back to campus, and in these heels." What was I even thinking?

"I could give you a ride," he suggests. "My car is just—"

"No." I shake my head at him. "Thank you for the offer but I will just text my sister to come down and we can Uber back. It makes the most sense, really."

Time to put a stop to this…flirtation…or whatever it is. Agreeing to let him walk me two miles back to campus was stupid. I blame the intoxicating scent of cologne and *him* clinging to his jacket for impairing my judgment.

"Okay, I can wait until she gets down here, then." Tyler does not seem the least bit discouraged by my refusal to go with him.

I send the text to Irina and Pam, then open the app to request a ride. "It says the car will be ten minutes."

"Damn, usually the cars don't take so long," Tyler says in that now recognizable Boston accent. The word cars comes out as *cahs*. I like it, *I think*, then mentally give myself a shake-down for liking anything about this arrogant hockey boy who is very clearly only interested in getting in my panties. I may be innocent about sex, but it does not mean I am naïve. "There must another event tonight or something else going on."

"It is okay. It will give my sister a moment to get down here."

We stand in awkward silence for a few minutes. I start to open my mouth to tell him he can go inside, that I will be fine, but then he asks, "What do you like to do for fun, Zoya Kolochev?"

"For fun?" I'm caught off guard by the question, as no one else tonight asked something so…personal. *About me.* "Well, I like yoga. And I paint occasionally. I am not very good, but it is calming. I also volunteered at a local animal shelter back home in Russia. I could do that here, I suppose."

I sense that none of those hobbies are on Tyler Lockhardt's list of "fun things." He has a gravelly voice and looks like walking sin. I know he is exactly the wild and undisciplined man my father wants me to stay far, far away from. And I would be happy to do so, honestly, if the car would just come already. Though there is that teeny, tiny piece of me that finds him slightly alluring.

"Painting, yoga, and animal welfare. All respectable uses of one's time."

"What about you?" I attempt making small talk with him. "What do you like to do for fun?"

"Ah, well, nothing as noble as what you just listed," he chuckles. "I would be happy to take you out and show you the city sometime, though. Since you're new to the area."

"Oh, that's very kind of you, but no, thank you."

"No, thank you?" By the incredulous look on his face and the raised eyebrows, Tyler Lockhardt must be used to getting his way most of the time.

"It is just that I really hoped to get a break from all things hockey while I was here. You see, my father is a hockey coach. My brother and my cousin, Boris, have played for a long time. We traveled all the time when I was younger, to and from their games. So much hockey in fact, I really want very little to do with the sport now."

"Well, we don't have to talk about hockey at all. There are plenty of other things to check out here—"

I shake my head again. "Sorry. No. You seem like a nice enough guy, Tyler, but I just think we have nothing much in common. I have lived my life around hockey, and now I will avoid it if I can. Your job involves lots of games and a lot of travel. I wish you the best with it, but I am not interested in that...*lifestyle* in my life right now. I hope you can understand."

Tyler looks dumbfounded. Thankfully, this conversation is over because my sister walks out of the arena just as the car pulls up at the curb. The problem of turning him down has been solved for me.

I inhale one last time before pulling his jacket from my shoulders and handing it back to him.

Why did you just do that?

Without a word he takes his jacket and steps down from the curb to open the car door for us. Irina holds up a pen and does a little dance before writing her number on Tyler's hand.

"Call me sometime, Tyler. We'll go make mischief together. I need a recommendation for a good tattoo artist. And someone to hold my hand when I'm getting it done." She kisses him on the cheek before sliding into the seat next to me.

As the door shuts, I say, "Slut."

"I heard that it is Tyler who is the slut." Irina nudges me in the shoulder. "Just my type."

I roll my eyes at her. "He will forget your name before he walks back inside. Why let him use you like that?"

"Oh, don't be such a nun. And who says it's just him using me? You don't need to be so prim and proper all the time. It's just sex, Zoya. And Tyler is super hot. Who wouldn't want to take him to bed?"

"Well me, for one. I have never taken any man to bed, and I certainly will not start with a fuck-boy hockey player."

For some reason, this just cracks my sister up. She laughs and laughs, but her only words are, "Get a life."

I am done talking about it, so I keep silent for the rest of the ride back.

But my sister's words stick with me and I cannot shake them off. I was sent to America to get an education. That is my purpose, and yet often when I speak with Irina about my choices and dreams, I sense that she looks at me with sympathy in her eyes. As if I'm so different to her that I'm somewhat... less. *Not as outgoing. Not as interested in sleeping with a super-hot man.* Not being me. Is that what she means? Am I that uninteresting?

Get a life. That is what I thought I was doing.

8
keep it movin'

Tyler

Smokeshow totally shut me down.

Damn.

Guess it'll have to be Irina, then. She's hot, too, so that's fine, I suppose. We'll go out and get her tattooed, and then I'll get her into bed. Score one for America. And, you know maybe a couple of scores for Russia, too. The female orgasm is real, and I'm generally an avid contributor to the cause.

I throw my jacket over my shoulder and catch the gentle trail of Zoya's perfume. I breathe in a deeper whiff and feel a stab of something unpleasant hit me right in the upper chest.

Weird.

The lush floral fragrance sticks with me all the way back up to the mid-season press party for some reason. Maybe because I keep turning my head toward my shoulder and sniffing for it. The scent of Zoya Kolochev on my jacket is way more addicting than it should be. This I *know*.

Big Brother Kolochev accosts me right off the bat.

"Stay away from my sisters, Lockhardt." He's literally pointing his finger right into my face. "I am not kidding."

I put my hands up. "Dude, I was just helping them get a ride home. Chill out. The younger one was bored out of her mind."

"My sisters are not for your entertainment," he says, then makes the universal two-finger signal for *I'm watching you.* "I want them far, far away from guys like you."

This cracks me up. "Guys like me? May I remind you that before you met your wife, you were exactly the same. We went out together, dude. I know what you did. And you might have been even worse than me, if we're really analyzing behaviors."

"That may be the case, but I still don't want you near my sisters. Don't even look at them. They are off limits. O.F.F. Got it?"

I can't help but roll my eyes at this guy. All protective when, not too long ago, he would've screwed two hot chicks faster than you could order a value meal at McDonald's. It wouldn't have mattered if they were the Pope's daughters. It wouldn't have mattered if they were any other NHL player's sisters either. He had no moral fiber, and yet he attacks mine. *Hypocrite.* Lucky for me, he won't be able to guard them at every turn, but I'll appease him, given I have to play with him and he's a bitch on the ice when he doesn't get his way.

"Whatever, bro. I was just being a gentleman. There are plenty of fish in the sea."

Pam wanders back to Georg's side, finally, but he's still in a complainy mood. "You were supposed to give the girls a ride home."

"Sorry. I got distracted by a tiny, pink human. Baby Alex was just too sweet to resist," Pam says dreamily.

Georg isn't having any of it. "Well, they had to get a ride service. And they had to hang out with Tyler Numbnuts for a while."

"I'm sure it wasn't all that bad. Tyler can be quite charming when he wants to be. And they are adults, Georg. They're capable of riding two miles in a taxi cab."

"Well, you said you would do it."

Pam gives him big eyes. "Well, I'm not your personal assistant. You could have driven them home yourself, too. I felt like holding the baby, and I do what I please, thank you very much."

"My father told me to keep an eye on them." Georg just can't let it go.

"Your father is an overprotective, old-fashioned man. The girls are grownups now and they're looking for freedom. They need room to explore. They'll be fine."

"Tell my father that," Georg mumbles under his breath.

This marital spat is boring. And fucking uncomfortable with me standing right here listening to it. Things like this are reason *numero uno* that I will never, ever fall in love or get in a relationship or whatever. They don't even notice when I drift away from them.

I head back over to my tree trunk of a best friend. He and Scarlett are cooing over their baby, who they named after both of their fathers. Alexander Michael is his name and I made sure to carve it in stone in my brain. Friends and family, I make an effort for. Alex is a cute baby as babies go. Probably gonna be a brick shithouse like his dad. I swear, the guy is a stone façade until he's around his kid. Then he turns into a really fucking large pile of mush.

"How was that?" Vik asks smugly.

"Georg was pretty clear about his feelings. Which means I got good and *briefed!* about how I need to stay away from his sisters."

"I told you so."

"Yep, you told me so, big guy. Georgie doesn't want his sisters defiled by icky hockey players."

"Well, family should be off limits anyway," Scarlett chimes in. "I think I'm team Georg with this one, Tyler. There are plenty of bunnies who will hop right onto your carrot with very few repercussions. Certainly, they won't have the family baggage that those two would. You should just shake it off and move on."

I narrow my eyes at her. "I will remember that, Red, the next time you want me to cooperate on some dumb-ass social media thing."

"Oh, don't be such a sore loser. You can't have every pretty girl you see. Jesus, Tyler, let it go." Vik stands there and smirks as his wife scolds me. No help from either of them coming my way on this.

Whateva.

Now I'm salty. Not at Red. I mean, I get it. Stay away from sisters and from family in general. Fine. But I've had enough of this party and this monkey suit. I've sure as hell had enough of being told to back off from the Kolochev sisters. I don't act any damn different from any of these other assholes, yet I'm the one getting told to step away and keep it movin'.

I need to get out of here.

I'll start banging my head against the wall soon if I don't get somewhere with low lighting, willing women, and plentiful alcohol. See there? I'll just go find myself another tall, brunette distraction.

As I told Georg, there are plenty of fish in the sea.

There are, yes.

But fuck. It's not going to be so easy to forget the one who was wearing my jacket tonight. *Smokeshow.*

Dumb-ass move giving it to her, because, shit, she smells fucking fine.

Move along now, Locksey. Time for some fishing.

9

perhaps you need a tutor?

Zoya

February

"Kak nash rebenok?" my mom squeals through the phone. Her face looks pixelated due to the time difference and likely poor cell coverage from where she's at. Still, I am happy to see her.

"English, Mama," I remind her. "We all need the practice. And I am not a baby."

"You are still your mother's baby," my father scolds, standing behind her shoulder. "Are you being good? Staying away from the party crowd?"

"Of course, I am, Papa. Irina is another story, though."

"As always," my dad says. Then he mutters, "*Bol'shaya problema.*"

Big trouble. Well, he's not wrong there.

"How is dorm room?" Mama asks, her English jerky.

I flip the screen so they can see the room while I tell them about how Georg paid to get me a private room. My father grumbles again in Russian, something along the lines of, "*On tratit slishkom mnogo deneg.*" Translation? My brother spends too much money. He is hard to hear in the background, but it would be right on point for him. Papa is a frugal man and my brother is not, and never has been. Still, he leans in and says he is glad I am able to have my own space and he thinks I must be safer that way.

Safety—always my father's primary concern.

"You are make friends?" Mama asks.

"Yes. I mean, it has only been a couple of weeks but so far, things are good. There is a guy in one of my classes, Jay, who seems nice."

"A man?" Papa booms in the background.

I roll my eyes at my mom and she giggles. "Just a friend, Papa. I think I need to get a job or volunteer somewhere. I might be able to meet some people. Or join a club. I have not decided."

"Is there a Russian heritage group or something?" he asks.

I scrunch one side of my face at the thought. "Why would I want to hang out with a bunch of Russian people, Papa? I just left Russia."

"Safer for you, my Zoya. How are your studies? Focus on grades first, social life second."

"They are mostly good. It is very early in the semester. There is plenty of time."

"Do not fall behind. You are there to learn."

"Yes, Papa. I know this. I am committed."

"Good girl. Mama and I are proud of you."

"I struggle with my statistics class," I admit.

"Oh, I am good at statistics," Papa says.

"You should be. Coaching all these years."

"Perhaps you need a tutor?"

A shrug is all I can give him in response. I have never needed a tutor before this class. Maybe it is because my classes are all in English now.

"Get one if you need one. Do not let yourself get too far behind."

"I won't."

Then he says, "Well, maybe having a job or volunteer role might keep you away from the party scene."

I have to laugh at him. "Have you ever met me?" I never party, and they know that. My sister, on the other hand?

My father seems to remember who he is talking to, because he says, "We should probably call and check in on Irina."

A huff of a laugh escapes me. "Uh, yeah. Though good luck trying to control that one."

"Is she being bad?" Mama asks.

"She is being Irina," I answer. "I think she likes it here, though. Feminist heaven."

My mom makes a confused face. She does not understand the "feminist heaven" part. My father does, though, based on the smirk on his face. He stops smirking when I tell a story about how Irina got in a shouting match with a man on the street who was harassing a prostitute. My father is, of course, mortified and says he's going to call Georg and have him keep a better eye on us.

"Georg is busy, Papa. He has his own life and he is in season. Everyone loves him here. They love the team."

My father relaxes the minute I start talking hockey. He asks if I have been to a game and I say no, but that we went to a mid-season press event and met a lot of the players and staff. He says I should at least go to one game to cheer on my brother.

"He would like it," Mama agrees. "To see you on the seats."

"It is fun to watch a winning team, Zoya," Papa adds. "The crowd will be loud. It will be fun."

"I have had enough hockey fun to last my whole life, thank you. Georg can live without having me in the stands."

"One game, Zoya," my father says sternly.

"Okay, okay. Fine. I will go to one game. But for now, I need to get going on some homework. Did I mention I hate my stats class?"

"No, you say trouble," my mother says. "No hate."

"Okay, I greatly dislike the class because it is giving me trouble. How is that, Mama?"

"Better. Get tutor."

We talk for a few more minutes but then I insist I need to get off the phone to study. It is getting late there, so they agree to let me go. I know they miss seeing us. I miss them, but honestly, only having to *report in* over the phone is much nicer than being watched over my shoulder every day. Papa is like any other Russian father—protect family at all costs. It is all he knows. It is all I know. But with the feeling of freedom alive in Vegas, I am enjoying being away from home right now...so much more than I thought I would. Even though Mama's eyes looked sad as I said goodbye, I know *getting a life* in Vegas will make her proud and happy. *This is for you, Mama.* But it is also for me.

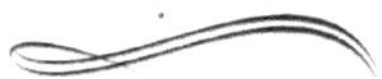

I AM ALLOWED EXACTLY twenty minutes of quiet study time before my sister barges through my door, her eyes bright and an excited smile lighting up her face.

"Come with me. I'm getting my first tattoo today!"

"Papa is going to murder you, Rina."

"He will not. It will be fine."

"He is going to call you. I just hung up with him and Mama twenty minutes ago."

"Well, you don't have to answer just because they call," she says.

"That is rude. They are our parents. They pay our tuition."

"Whatever. Are you coming with me or not?"

"I have so much work to do—"

"Don't be such a drag. I need you there with me."

I make a face but then get up and pull on some jeans and an oversized, black T-shirt. I twist my hair up into a messy bun and slip on a pair of lemon-yellow Keds. Irina bounces impatiently while I get ready, and the second I look presentable, she grabs my hand and literally tows me from my room. At least that has been consistent since I arrived. Irina pulling me toward something drama-filled.

"I hope you will not end up regretting this, Rina."

"I never regret, little sister. Never."

10
will this hurt?

Tyler

I'm leaning against the glass window of the tattoo shop where I've gotten the last three of my own tats. Irina asked me for a recommendation and while there are a lot of world-class artists in Vegas, there are like four times as many shitty ones. And I don't need one more reason for Brother Georg to be pissed at me. Once he finds out his sister and I have been texting, despite his clear orders to stay far away, he'll blow a gasket. Adding in a bad tattoo would only be causing more fucking hassle for me. My face is too pretty to be beaten by a Kolochev-size fist.

Honestly, I wasn't going to text her anymore when she said she wanted to get her first tattoo. I really wasn't. I was gonna be the good boy, the adult in the room, and stay away as asked. But when she sent me the name of a shop that I know is a total tourist trap, I couldn't in good conscience let her go there. See? I was doing a good thing. I mean, I suppose one could argue I could've made the recommendation and then walked away. I didn't *have* to agree to come in person for her appointment. Still, I consider it a humanitarian aid mission. She's from another country. I don't want her to get ripped off or worse. A tat gone bad is a serious deal.

A car pulls up and Irina shoots out like a ball from a cannon. I'm immediately enveloped in a giddy hug, and I'm so dumbfounded that I almost miss the additional person who exits the car, casual and effortless with her hair piled on top of her head and supersized sunglasses that nearly cover half her face.

I couldn't tell you what Irina is wearing. My sights are fixed on Zoya, clearly uncomfortable and maybe somewhat disapproving, her lips down in a model's pout. Goddamn. I am certain I've never seen a more beautiful woman.

"Hey, ladies," I say as Irina steps back a bit bouncing on her heels excitedly.

"Thank you *so* much for setting this up," Irina says, her grin wide.

I shrug. "My pleasure. I had to use my pro-athlete status to get you in on a Sunday, though. They usually book several months out, but I've spent a lot of money in here, so they made a special time."

Irina's grin just gets wider. Zoya, however, looks totally unimpressed. She still hasn't said a word. Not even a hello.

We wander inside and I introduce them to Erik,

the artist. A massive Swede with an inclination for all things goth, he asks Irina about her interests and sketches a few things as they talk. She wants something empowering, which is no surprise to me at all.

I notice Zoya perusing the wall of flash art and wander over, leaving Irina and Erik to figure out the design since I have no input to provide about feminist imagery.

"See anything you like?" I ask from behind her.

She stays facing the art wall. "No. This is all generic."

"You're right. Flash is meant to be a quick money-maker. Most people want custom ink on their bodies, something no one else has. To get that, you pay more, and it usually takes more time to prep and do the work."

"I doubt I would ever get one, anyway," she says with a soft shake of her head. "They are not for me."

I think of my own highly tattooed body and wonder if she would find my ink unattractive. For the first time ever—seriously, ever—I feel kinda self-conscious about my body art. Usually women find it sexy and I sure as hell like how it looks. But here's this one woman, who clearly doesn't give a shit about me, and I'm seriously rethinking former my life choices. At least, as it relates to tattoos.

"Yo, Lockhardt," Erik calls over to me as he draws. "You on the road soon? Due for some away games since you've been at home the last few, yeah?"

"Yep. We have a four-game roadshow coming up. We're in Jersey, New York, Boston, and Philly."

"Oh, you are from Boston, right?" Irina asks. "Will you get to see family while you are there?"

"Thought you were spawned from the underworld, yo," Erik says with a chuckle. "You got a family?"

"You're not so far off on that one, brother. But I mean, maybe. Yeah. I guess I might try to see them while I'm in town."

Erik and Irina both eye the design he's come up with. Irina proclaims it perfect and holds it up for Zoya to see. Zoya gives a half-hearted thumbs up then comments on the fact that the flower in the design is the Russian national flower, which looks like a little yellow daisy to me.

Design done, Erik goes to get everything set up, having Irina lie face down on his table. She's getting the tattoo on her lower back, presumably so she can hide it easily from her parents. *Not sure if I should tell her that it's considered a tramp stamp.*

"Will this hurt?" Irina gives me a grimace from the table.

"Probably," I tell her. "That part of your back can be sensitive. But the pain is more like getting stung by a bee a bunch of times. It's more of an annoyance than real pain. You know what I mean? It'll be like a sunburn while it heals."

"Hold my hand while he does it?" Irina thrusts her hand at me, so I fold my much larger one around hers. All I feel is delicate cold skin. Her hand holds no heat at all.

But before Erik even has the stencil placement set onto Irina's back, my phone starts blowing up. It's my mom. Ugh. I cringe and hit the "decline" button to send it to voice mail. Zoya sits on a stool next to her sister as my mom calls back again about two minutes later. And then again, another couple minutes after that. *Fucking great.*

"Your sister will have to step in, sorry." I hold up my phone. "I gotta take this."

As I step outside into the sunlight I pick up. "Ma."

"Tyler," she barks into my ear, "can't answer the first time I call?"

"I was busy. Whattaya need?"

"You think I only call when I need somethin'?" She sounds...wounded for lack of a better term. I hear the flick of a lighter and an inhale as she lights her cigarette. The sound instantly takes me to a dark place and fills my gut with anxiety.

"I would say ninety-nine percent of the time, yeah. You doin' okay?"

"Well, my welfare check won't be comin' on time this month. Somethin' got messed up at the office and now I gotta go fill out new paperwork. It's a whole headache I don't need right now."

"Sorry to hear that, Ma."

"You know," she says, her voice going all up and down like she's trying to cry, "it's never easy for me. With these two mouths to feed, it can get hard. And you're out there livin' the high life."

"Yeah, I've got a job playin' hockey. What's that got to do with your situation? Just go in and fill out the paperwork." *Or, you know, go out and get a job yourself.*

"It ain't that simple, son. I go in and then they gotta review it and then they gotta go, like, eat seven donuts at Dunkies, and then they gotta think about it. It takes forever. And in the meantime, I get no check and can't get groceries."

"I don't know what you want me to do, Ma." *I do know. It's the exact reason I don't want to pick up her calls. Money. Always fucking money.*

"You're a rich, famous athlete, aren't you? You've got money to burn on booze and your whores. You can help your family, surely!"

"You know, I hate it when you try and guilt me like this. I've given you plenty over the years. Tens of thousands. Rent on a nice place to live and you trashed it and got kicked out. Money in a bank account for the kids, and you spent it all. Got you a car so you could get back and forth to work and then you got fired and sold it. Do I need to go on, Ma? Do I?"

My head hurts. This is what conversations with my mom are like. Every time.

She whines into the phone. "What about your brother and sister, though?"

I blow out a long breath and push my hands through my hair. I'd like to rip it out, this is so frustrating. Logan and Haley. My four- and six-year-old half brother and sister. Even though they have the same last name as me, we only share a mother. No clue who their father/s is/are.

Also, the only reason I pick up when my mother calls.

And ninety percent of the reason I keep shelling out coin.

The other ten percent? My Ma. She did give me life after all, so I love her for that. She's had a hard go. *I* had a hard go until I got away from that life. Darlene Lockhardt has been in and out of treatment three times for drugs over the years. She's had men in and out of her life, most of them heavy drinkers and abusers who made life even worse for her. And she's got two little kids to show for it; kids I'm not always convinced she really wants. I think she likes getting extra money from welfare each month, though she sure as hell doesn't use it to make their lives better. I'll never tell her—*I don't trust her for shit*—but I set up two trust funds for them so they can go to college someday, make something of themselves. *Get away from the mess that is my ma.* Theirs too. *Poor kids.*

She goes on and on about how hard it is, crying and getting more and more hysterical. I sit on the curb, head in my hands, ready to throw my phone across the road.

"Everything you're tellin' me right now just makes me think I should call my lawyer and get custody of the kids."

She laughs, a sharp, shrill sound. "That's about as likely as hell freezin' over, kid. You can barely take care of yourself. You're like an overgrown teenager with your hand up every girl's skirt. You take to the bottle as much as anyone else. What the hell's the court gonna see in you that's better than their own mother?"

"Uh, I have a stable income and a home that doesn't have cockroaches crawling in and outta the cupboards. Oh, and I don't have a string of abusive assholes rolling in and out of their lives through a revolving door."

"No, you just got a cupboard full of liquor and a different whore in your bed every night. That's much better. You're such a hypocrite. Barely an adult yourself! You don't know shit about takin' care of kids. And get off your high horse. Just 'cause you got money now don't mean you're better than me. You're still just trash from Southie and that's never gonna change, son."

"I didn't say I was better than you, Ma, just more stable."

"But I'm stable," she protests. "I got a little part-time job. I'm tryin', son, I really am tryin'. I lost weight. It's better now. I just need a boost this month while the paperwork gets sorted out. Just a little to stay afloat, son."

A sound escapes the back of my throat, somewhere between a growl and a groan. "Fine. I'll wire some money, but you better use it on food, not drugs."

"Thanks, Tyler. You're good to—"

"I'm done," I growl then hang up. *Fuck. Me.* Why?

You're such a hypocrite. Barely an adult yourself! You don't know shit about takin' care of kids.

Well, fuuuck.

Ma's not wrong.

I'm *not* the best role model for Logan and Haley.

I'm just another pro-athlete who travels all the time and rarely has an evening at home. A guy who spends his free time drinking and fucking his way through North America. Not a newsflash to anyone. This story's been told time and time again in every professional sport by a thousand different guys. That I just happen to be the NHL's wild child of the moment? Okay fine, ya got me. But what's so wrong about any of that for a single guy on his own?

Which I am.

I'm a regular guy trying to make something of his life.

A twenty-four-year-old dude who invests way more than I spend. I set up trust funds for Haley and Logan. I give money to charity. I'm not a bad person and I'm not an alcoholic. Drinking is social for me. It's not something I do alone or anything I require in my life. I could give those kids a home if I had to. I've got a three-bedroom place. A fridge stocked with healthy food. The means to provide for their needs in a clean and safe environment.

But fuck. What would I do with two small kids when I'm on the road all the time? I mean, they barely know me. I hardly ever see them, and usually only on FaceTime. Christ. This situation sucks balls. *But do I want them? Do I want the responsibility?*

I groan again, just as Zoya sits down beside me on the curb.

"Are you okay?" Her voice is so soft. It nearly calms me, the sound of her soft words.

"I'm fine." I frown at the ground.

"Your body language seemed very tense while you were talking. I saw you from inside and now I can hear you are frustrated. It is unlike the way I have come to know you."

"What way have you come to know me?" I am genuinely intrigued.

"Cocky. Not serious. Interested in only sex."

"Well, I'm still those things too."

"I do not think that is true. Or at least is not the whole truth."

"Your English is really good."

She gives me a look like, *Really*. "You changed the subject. And yes, the English is good because I study every day, and I travel all the time to many places where English is a common tongue."

"What does it say about me that the only word I heard just now was tongue?" I tilt my head and grin at her, trying to crack a joke, make things normal.

"You are trying to blow this off. I promise I am a good listener, Tyler. I think there is more to you than what you share with people, and I am offering for you to share with me."

I bite the inside of my lip as I consider. I do not tell people about my family drama. Even Vik doesn't know. As far as anyone who knows me goes, I'm an orphan from the system with no family to speak of.

Do I want to share my crygasm with a woman who, twenty minutes ago, would barely speak to me?

Looking into her brown eyes flecked with gold, full of compassion and curiosity, I decide that I do.

What the hell.

Rip that motherfucking Band-Aid right off and let my sob story flow.

11
mr. gunnersen

Zoya

Tyler pushes his lips out and his nostrils flare. It is a weird look; one I realize indicates he is not sure if he wants to trust me. I sit and wait, quietly, giving him time to decide.

My mama has often done that with Papa when he's silent and she wants him to talk. *She always gets her way.* She told me once that there are two reasons men are slower to communicate. Sometimes it takes men a while to formulate their thoughts and decide if they wish to share them or not. And sometimes, they are prideful and avoid sharing things until they trust in the person asking for answers. My guess is it is the latter with Tyler. He knows my brother, not me.

I watch him as he wrestles with whatever is going on inside his mind. Finally, he starts talking and I listen—hanging onto his every word—laced in that accent of his which fascinates me.

"I grew up in Southie, that's the slum area of Boston, right? With a single mom so it was just the two of us. My dad died when I was young, too young to really remember him clearly. He had a work accident or something but it's not anything my ma ever really shared with me in any great detail. And what was the point anyway? Can't mourn someone you don't really know or even remember."

He scratches the stubble on his chin and blows out a big breath. "There was a short time when things were kind of okay, like she had a decent job and stuff, but then I started to notice random guys over all the time. In and out of the house. Some of them left money after staying the night. Sex noises from her room and all that. And drugs. Lines of coke on the kitchen table. A haze of smoke throughout the house. All that nonsense. So, I was like eight or nine getting this life lesson about sex and crime and drugs, while making my own peanut butter sandwiches and putting myself on the school bus every day."

"That must have been so hard."

"I dunno. Shit, I didn't know any different. I knew I wanted to get to school, anything to be away from the whole mess. Took the long way home every afternoon. But I also cleaned the house. And went to the grocery store. I was like a little man, you know? My ma called me the man of the house, so I was always real puffed up, like I was really takin' care of shit."

Seeing this side of him makes me soften. I thought he was just a rowdy, privileged hockey boy but maybe there is more to him than I originally thought. It's surprising me that he feels comfortable sharing this with me, and I wonder if he has had this conversation before?

He puts both hands on the back of his head and sits back, looking up at the sky. "So, some of the guys who came around to get with my mom were rough with me. And then I started gettin' rough with kids at school. You know, the old abused becoming the abuser bullshit. I had a gym teacher who was like, 'whoa, kid, what the fuck?' He told me I needed an outlet for my aggression. Got me playing hockey. I didn't have shit to pay for skates or pads, but he got it all figured out for me."

"Your gym teacher sounds like a good guy." I try to imagine what he was like as a young boy living such an unsettled life and my heart cracks open for him. Whatever preconceived ideas I had about Tyler Lockhardt before today were only a small part of the story.

"He was. Mr. Gunnersen." Tyler bobs his head up and down and swallows hard. "I should go back and see the old guy, huh? Thank him and shit. I joined a youth hockey team like two years later and got hooked. Wouldn't have found any of this life I have now if not for him."

"Maybe you should thank him, then. You have obviously done well."

"I mean, I—I do send money to support the club I played for. I always send it anonymously, but in his honor. I hope maybe he knows someone cares about what he does—what he *did* for a lot of poor kids."

"Well, you are lucky you found something you love."

"Yeah. Yep. I started working in and around the rink to help pay for my ice time and equipment and shit. Hockey helped me channel all my angry energy and kept me out of that house. I traveled to games a lot when I played club hockey, so I got to stay in hotels and stuff. I felt like a fuckin' king, you know? And my skills on the ice got better and better, so when I was sixteen, I got picked for an all-star team and we played in a huge tournament. Recruiters saw me and talked to me about playing for their college teams. I got offered a scholarship from Minnesota and took it because I wanted to get as far the fuck away from Boston as possible. I could've played for Boston College but no way I was gonna play with the Richie Rich boys. Fuck that."

"Well, it is good you could get away. So, what was this today? Your mother, I am guessing?"

He makes a face. "It was, indeed, my mother. Asking for money. Again. Guilting me. Using my siblings to get to me. Same shit, different day."

"She asks you for money often?"

"Probably once every other month. And I've tried, Zoya. I've tried getting her a good place to live, tried using connections to get her jobs, tried making sure there's always money in the account. And she's just a user. You know? She doesn't appreciate shit and she's just like a money-sucking monster who doesn't care about anything other than her next score or high or whatever. But the kids are little, and I have no fucking clue if she's doing to them what she did to me. It never ends."

"I am so sorry, Tyler. It sounds like you have done your best to care for your family."

"God, you're so kind. So nice. I feel bad making you listen to this garbage." He stands up and holds out a hand to help me up, as well. "I should probably go hold your sister's hand like I said I would. Thanks for listening."

"No problem, Tyler."

We head inside and Tyler jogs to Irina's side, apologizing and saying he got an unexpected call from his mother. He comments on the progress of her tattoo, which I have to admit does look really nice.

"Where did you go?" my sister asks me.

"I went out to get some air. Something about the sound of the buzzing and the blood made me a little woozy." Sometimes it is an easy thing to lie to the ones you are the closest to. I just lied to my sister and I never do that.

Tyler gives me a relieved look and I know I did the right thing by not outing him for sharing something so personal. He nods and I nod back, and in that moment, something shifts between us. I catch his gaze and hold it, every ounce of me wanting him to know that it means something that he told me about his family, his childhood. It makes him more real to me, more human. *Not only a hockey player.*

He still seems awkward, his lips set in a scowl as he does some sort of transaction on his phone with one hand while still holding on to Irina's with the other. I want to ask if he is moving money around, sending his mother what she asked for, but I know it would embarrass him.

When the tattoo is finished, Irina is a little lightheaded, but happy with the final product. We finish up, thanking Erik for his time and his excellent work. As we are walking out, I can see the lines of stress on Tyler's face even as he jokes about being hungry enough to eat his own arm.

"Well, we could all go out to celebrate Irina's first tattoo," I suggest.

Irina spins to look at me. "You want to go out?"

"Well, it is dinner time, right? It is Sunday, though, so I am not sure what else might be—"

"This is Vegas," Tyler interrupts. "There's always somewhere to go. I know just the place."

12

smokeshow sandwich

Tyler

"Oh, this is only like two blocks from my apartment," Irina comments as we walk into the sports bar I picked.

We get a table and I order myself a beer. Irina orders some frilly girl drink and Zoya just orders a diet soda. The waitress, who's cute and petite and ginger, tells me I look familiar. I'm about ready to get my flirt on when I realize Irina and Zoya might not appreciate it.

"He is a pro-hockey player," Irina says, grabbing my arm in a weirdly proprietary way.

"Oh, you play for the Crush, right?" the waitress asks. "On the back line?"

"Yup, play defense. You a Crush fan?"

She grins. "I've been to a few games. Honestly, I wasn't that into it until I saw how many hot guys there are on the team. Your teammate? With the long hair? Whew!" She fans herself with her order notebook and gets a dreamy look on her face.

"Georg Kolochev?" Chicks love that dude's long hair for some reason that escapes me.

"Yes!"

Both Irina and Zoya groan.

"That one is our dumb brother," Irina says, sticking her finger down her throat.

Ginger laughs and says, "Well, I think he's way hot. And the way his wife proposed to him was so cute. Swoon city."

"Well, on that note, could I get a hamburger with lettuce, tomato, and pickle?" Zoya asks, ignoring the total fangirling this redhead is doing over her brother. "With fries on the side?"

We all order and when the waitress leaves, Zoya rolls her eyes. "I have no patience for any of that nonsense."

"I didn't think she was that bad," I say with a shrug. "So she thinks your brother's hot. So what?"

"It is all the time," Zoya says. "Everywhere. I cannot go to the bank without someone mentioning my brother or my cousin or the Crush or hockey. I have lived and breathed hockey for my whole life and now I am ready to talk about something else."

"This is her hot button," Irina comments. "Do not, under any circumstances, say the H word."

This makes me chuckle. I can understand it to some extent. Now that many of the guys are married or have girlfriends—and babies—I get just as irate when the conversation inevitably turns to those topics. Shaking my head in understanding, I drink some of my beer. "How's the back feeling?"

"Not too bad," Irina says. "A little sore, like a burn. Nothing I cannot handle."

"Take those bandages off when you get home. Make sure you keep a thin layer of ointment on it until it starts to dry out. It will scab up and peel, then you can put unscented lotion on it to keep it moist."

"Thank you, doctor," she says in a sultry voice. "I am thankful to have you to take good care of me."

Zoya snorts lightly on my other side. I look at her from the corner of my eye and see her smothering a laugh. She scoots out of the booth and says she needs to run to the restroom. It occurs to me that she's trying to avoid cockblocking her sister by laughing at her obvious flirtation. And if she doesn't want to cockblock, then does that mean I have no chance with her? I know it makes me sound like a genuine asshole, but I am *not* used to having women totally blow me off. I thought we had a moment back at the tattoo shop. I shared things with her that my best friend doesn't even know. I thought I saw something in her eyes, her expression...a new interest, maybe? And no, I didn't share my sad-sack life story with her to try for a pity fuck.

Hell, I don't know. Maybe I should chalk it as a loss. Irina is beautiful and totally interested. It won't amount to anything, as I can't risk pissing off Georg to the point that we can't play together.

Our food comes and we all chat about campus life. Zoya talks about her boring biology class and her frustration with her statistics class. Irina talks about a thesis idea she's working on before switching gears to talk about her two roommates.

"Solveig is from Norway, doing a PhD in physics. She's a fucking genius. And Willa is from South Africa. She's studying something to do with gender and athletics. I like them both, but I hardly ever see them. I don't think they ever stop working."

"Sounds interesting," is all I can think to say.

"I mean," Irina says, "that they are never home. I am always alone."

I turn and meet her gaze, which is full of invitation. Oh yeah. Instinctively, I look over at Zoya, who has her hamburger up to her mouth. Her eyes are wide and it's a pretty humorous sight, but I'd give anything to know what she's thinking. Is she shocked that her sister would be so forward? Or so forward with her still sitting here?

The urge to know what she's thinking and feeling is overwhelming for me. I shouldn't care. She's too young for me, anyway. Only nineteen, just a sophomore in college. I'll be twenty-five in a few months.

Irina's phone rings and she answers in Russian, then scoots out of the booth and toward the front of the restroom. I watch her go, then turn to Zoya again.

"Her ex-boyfriend," she explains. "Vladimir."

"Still a thing?"

"Who knows? She is fickle about these things." We're both quiet for a few moments, before she asks, "Are you going to sleep with my sister?"

I swear I almost choke on the bit of burger I've got

in my mouth. "Well, I—I mean, I—she seems like—maybe?" Holy shit, why am I stammering? And when did it get so hot in here? "It seems like she was maybe hinting—"

"She was more than hinting, Tyler. It was an open invitation. She is always direct about what she wants, and she wants to sleep with you. It will not mean anything, so you are in the clear. She will not hound you for more."

"Oh." I take that all in and chew on it for a second. "I mean, that's cool…I guess."

"I know this is how you operate. There is no reason to hide it."

I choke out a laugh. "Fair enough. Would you be upset? If I start something with your sister?" I sound so awkward. What is wrong with me? I feel weird and nervous and tongue-tied like some teenage kid with his first crush. *Christ, get yourself together, Lockhardt.*

She shrugs. "Why would I care?"

"I thought maybe you might not approve or whatever." I sound fucking lame, but I keep right on going. "I won't do it if you tell me you don't want me to."

"You are an adult. She is an adult. I have no say in what the two of you choose to do. You can have sex with each other if you like. Plus, I am not the sibling to worry about. If Georg finds out, beware." Zoya is prim, tight-lipped, as she says all this. And she's looking down at her plate, not at me. This bothers her; *I know it.*

Suddenly, Irina is back, and she starts by laying

out six shot glasses of what I'm guessing is top-shelf vodka on the table. "Fucking Vlad," she grumbles. "He makes me want to get drunk."

She pushes two shot glasses in front of me, two in front of her own seat, and two in front of Zoya.

"I do not drink," Zoya protests. "I am not of age."

"Oh, live a little," Irina scolds. "You are of age in Russia and have had alcohol, so stop acting like a nun."

They stare at each other and I see something in Zoya's face change. The challenge has been accepted, I guess. She tosses the first shot back, making a sour face as her sister hoots with delight. The two of us follow by taking our shots, as well.

We eat a bit more before we do the second shot. I buy us a third round. It's starting to get fun here. Zoya, a bit woozy now, is loosening up, telling funny stories about her brother when he was a kid.

She slaps her hands on the table at one point and exclaims, "We should go dancing!"

"It is Sunday," Irina says. "Are there places open?"

"Always. Remember it's Vegas, baby." I throw my credit card on the table and the waitress pops over to get us paid up. "And dancing is my middle name."

"That is a weird middle name," Zoya comments.

"Ever use contractions?" I ask her, all loose-lipped, finally feeling comfortable enough to tease her.

Zoya tilts her head in question.

Irina says, "When you mush two words together. *That's a weird middle name*, instead of *that is a weird middle name.* The way you use English makes you sound very stiff."

"I have been told my English is very good." Zoya pushing her lips out in a pout makes me want to kiss her right there and then, I swear.

"It is," I reassure her. "Really good."

We head out, piling into a car for a ride that takes less than five minutes. It's still early, but there are some people dancing in the small club when we walk in. We're all a little loaded, so we don't care that the place isn't hopping yet.

We just make our way over to the dance floor and in no time, I'm the filling in a sexy Russian smokeshow-sandwich.

Best Sunday night ever.

13
wakey wakey

Zoya

I am not a prude, not really. I have been at parties with my friends back home. Had drinks a few times, a hit of marijuana occasionally. It is more I do not—*don't* like feeling out of control, and that is very nearly what I feel now. I can still think, but the alcohol has lifted many of my barriers. Which is not a good thing, but being here, dancing, seems okay, at least for now.

Irina is sexy dancing for Tyler, her front to his front, her hips to his hips. Being the more reserved, less experienced one, I am behind him, my front to his back, my hands just barely on his hips, my movements mirroring his. I am like a shadow. It is awkward and funny and probably not at all sexy, but he does not seem to mind. He is smiling a lot, his hands resting on Irina's waist, sometimes moving up to the edge of her breasts. If he moved his thumbs, he could brush them over her nipples, which are hard beneath her soft T-shirt.

She wants him, and something about their exchange makes me feel a way that I am—*I'm* not sure how to describe. I'm not a very good dancer; rhythm *doesn't* come naturally to me. While the alcohol makes me feel looser, it also makes me more aware of my insecurities. I'm not confident with men. I'm not experienced. I don't know how to be sexy or capture a man's attention.

I think about Tyler, about his upbringing, and I feel like he has given me something special by sharing with me. Knowing this about him makes me feel like he trusts me, and I like that. I like it a lot actually, much to my complete surprise.

But I don't want to like Tyler Lockhardt. He is everything I don't want in my life. He parties. He uses women. He is all about hockey. I will admit he is really cute, handsome in a rugged way. He calls us smokeshows, which means a hot, sexy female. But I feel like the term should refer to guys as well. Tyler is the male version of a smokeshow to me.

I like the way his biceps fill out his shirt sleeves. I like the way his blond hair flops in his face. I like his five-o-clock shadow. Yes, I find him attractive...but still, I want a normal guy. A prince charming type, who will sweep me off my feet. I don't want a hockey guy, a wham-bam guy who takes my virginity and runs away with it.

No, I want my first time to be special. Meaningful. Would it be, were I to share that first time with a guy like Tyler? I don't have the answer to that question.

I want to unload all of this to the bartender when I

take a break for water, trying to clear my head of the swishy feelings I am—*I'm* having. Instead, I only tell her it is my sister over there dancing with the man I am interested in.

It's just the alcohol, nothing more, and if I can get back to a more sober state, I will realize that Irina and Tyler make sense. They will dance, then they will have sex, and then we will probably never see Tyler again, unless it's on the ice.

"Sounds like a tough one," the bartender says.

We both look out to the dance floor, which has a few more people on it than when we arrived. Irina and Tyler are still out there, having fun. She has her back to him and literally slithers up and down in front of him, his hands all over her. There is no way they will not have sex tonight.

I cannot feel like this. I cannot care. No, *I'll* just be his friend. My sister can do what she will with him. Yes, *that's* the best choice here.

"I need to get out of here," I announce, even though the bartender has moved on to another customer.

I order a ride, which comes quickly. Inside the car, I send my sister a text, telling her I'm fine but tired and heading back to the dorm.

Back in my dorm, I strip down to just my black T-shirt and panties before crashing onto the bed, exhausted. I check my phone just once as my eyelids get heavy. There are no texts from my sister, which makes me think she and Tyler are either still on the dance floor, or they have made their way to her apartment.

To fuck.

I should not—*shouldn't* care, but there is a bit of an ache in my belly when I think of how they looked while they danced. She was confident and sexy. He was strong and attractive. They looked happy.

But then I always see Irina that way. When guys look at her and she gets angry, there is always that quick look of satisfaction on her face. *She loves the attention. Knows what to do with it.* And of course, why wouldn't Tyler look at her exactly as every other man does? You need to be sexy, gregarious. *Something I am not. Nor ever will be.*

Yet as much as I try to deny it, I wish Tyler had looked at me that same way. Even if for one moment. One night.

A LOUD BANGING on the door wakes me up.

Not even aware I'd fallen asleep; I find myself confused. What time is it? I look at my phone and see it's past two in the morning. I wander to the door, still half asleep, and find Tyler standing there, hulking in my doorway looking like sin and wonder.

"Tyler? Is everything okay? Is Irina—"

"Your sister's fine." *Sistah.* That accent. Oh boy. "She was totally blitzed, so I took her home, fed her some aspirin, made her drink some water, and then put her to bed. Alone."

"So why are you here?" I ask, still groggy. "How are you here? How did you know where my room was?"

"The last thing Irina said to me before passing out was that I was to come over here and make sure you got home okay. You bailed without saying goodbye. Everything okay?"

"Oh." Suddenly I feel shy, but I decide to tell him the truth anyway. "I just felt like an extra. Do you know what I mean? What is the expression?"

"Third wheel?"

"Okay. Yes?"

"Like on a bicycle. They have two wheels. A third doesn't make sense."

"Ah." I lick the front of my teeth which feel utterly gross. "Excuse me for a second?"

I grab my toiletry kit and walk down the hall to the bathroom where I can wash my face and brush my teeth.

Which is stupid because I should just send him on his way. It's late and I'm tired. And he said he only came over because Irina told him to. What does it matter if I have bad breath and the remnants of yesterday's mascara smudged under my eyes?

It's not like I will be kissing him tonight.

Right?

14
zoned

Tyler

Thank God she's gone for a second. Seeing her like that, her hair loose around her shoulders, her lids heavy from sleep, in her tiny panties and tight T-shirt. Holy hell, Zoya has no idea what she looks like to me right now.

She has reallllly long legs and reallllly pretty skin and I'm not drunk, so I feel secure in saying that I am dead certain I have never seen a more beautiful woman than Zoya Kolochev.

When she comes back, she sits on her bed and pats the spot beside her. I sit, feeling oddly nervous and stiff.

"I'm glad you are here, Tyler." Her voice is so soft and sweet. It's like cotton candy.

"Really?"

"I wanted to tell you that I'm glad you trusted me enough to tell me your story earlier."

"Oh." I wave off the comment. "It's no biggie."

"I think it is, *a biggie,* as you say. I think you try to play tough guy, like you don't care about anything, but it's because of everything you have gone through. You had to fight to get out of the life handed to you. Maybe, I think, you need a friend to talk to sometimes."

"I have friends," I say, running a hand through my hair. I feel disgusting, all of a sudden, sweaty from dancing, alcohol still on my breath. And yes, Irina's kisses on my lips. She wanted me. And fuck, I was tempted. Kissed her. But... but here I am. With a girl who saw me. Now talking 'bout my friends.

"But do you have people you can talk to? About important things?"

I start to say yes, but in the end, I have to admit I don't have that in my life. I never really have. My "friendships" were surface level in college and with teammates over the years. Viktor is the first true friend I've had, and I don't even tell him about my crazy mother. I shake my head no.

Zoya reaches over and takes my hand in hers. I stare at it, my big, clunky dude hand holding her petite, delicate one. "Well, I declare that we are now best friends, Tyler Lockhardt. I'm going to be that person for you."

I stare at her, dumbfounded. She wants to be my BFF? I almost laugh, because it feels hysterical to want someone as badly as I want her, only to be told that we are now best friends and I am to share all of my innermost feelings with her. When all I really want is to kiss her until she goes blind with desire.

"What if…" I start, pursing my lips and letting a breath out through my nose. "What if I want more?"

"More?"

"Than just friendship. With you."

Zoya blushes, and not just on her cheeks. Her whole chest blooms peach. But she says those same words I've heard before. "I don't want a hockey boy, remember? The fact I'm offering my friendship is a lot, because I don't really want hockey in my life either. But I like you and I think you need a friend. And I want to be that friend."

"But I—"

She shakes her head at me. "No, Tyler. I came here to study. I am too familiar with the truth of hockey life, and I therefore know it's not something I want to be part of. I will not date a hockey player."

"It's just that I find you very attractive, Zoya. What is it you're lookin' for in a guy? If it's not me, who is it?"

"I need a prince charming. Someone who will romance me. He will want to know everything about me. And buy me flowers. He will make me feel like love is a fairy tale made real."

A derisive noise comes out of me. I don't mean for it to, but it does, and she looks away, blushing again, embarrassed. I scramble to find words that will make it better. "You're a romantic, I get it. Maybe I could try to be that for you?"

She squeezes my hand. "No. That is not you. You are not built for that love. And I will not settle. Being your friend is all I can offer. I really want that for us. Do you?"

I think about it for a moment. She's not wrong. I've never been in love. Never even tried. Never wanted it. And yes, this woman is knocking my socks off in a way that women usually don't, but it doesn't mean I can suddenly morph into a Disney prince.

"Okay," I say finally. "You're right. I'd rather have you for a friend than nothing at all."

She smiles and it sinks my stomach. Fuck. I want to growl or cry or something because she is just so stinkin' amazing.

"Though I've never had a friend who's a girl," I add. "I might be a shitty friend. In fact, there's a really good possibility of that."

"But I believe in you, Tyler." She stands, towing me up off the bed. Pushing up on her tiptoes, she kisses me on the cheek before wrapping her arms around my midsection for a hug. I put my hands around her too, wanting desperately to touch the silky-smooth skin showing at her hips. I rest my head on top of hers and we just hold each other for a moment. It feels really fucking good.

When I pull away, I give her a cheeky grin.

"What?" she asks sweetly.

"Well, since we're BFF's now, does that mean I can't bang your sister?"

"Nope," she says, one side of her lips pulling up. "You can bang my sister to your heart's content. As long as she consents."

I salute her, and then head out the door, shutting it and leaning back, trying to catch my breath. I pull my shirt up over my nose, trying to catch the scent of her there, but of course, all I can smell is sweat and Irina. She was all over me for hours, so that makes sense. *Would Zoya mind if I grab a clean shirt and go back for a hug?*

I then roll my eyes at myself.

Best friends, indeed. I push off, adjust the semi I'm sporting, and head out, wishing I lived in an alternate universe where I could be more than just this woman's friend.

15
she's something

Zoya

I lie down on my bed, still smelling Tyler all over me. I feel the scratch of his beard against my cheek, the callouses on his hands. His strong arms wrapped around me, his broad chest against mine, our hearts beating wildly. Even though we had only hugged for a few seconds, because of his height, I had felt small. *It had felt so nice.*

Why do I feel like this? Uncomfortable. Achy. Unsettled. I try closing my eyes in meditation. I try breathing. In and out. Slowly. Mindfully. Nothing works.

When I think of him, I feel...desire. It is desire I feel, the hot ache unspooling low in my belly, making my toes curl. I toss and turn, trying to make the feeling go away. I tell myself that this is best. No hockey players for me. No hockey in my life at all. I want something different, someone different. A guy like Tyler is bound to hurt me, and then I would have given in for nothing.

Plus, he needs a good friend. He needs someone stable, someone he can talk to. And Irina likes him a lot. She wants him.

Still, the thoughts of his body, his smell, his touch...they swirl in my head and I find my hand snaking down beneath the soft cotton of my panties. I imagine it was me on that dance floor. Me that he looked at with desire, caressed, rubbed his body seductively against. I gasp, shocked at how wet I am down there. Wet with want. Need. Desire.

My fingertips play at the wet folds of my pussy, pushing to find the small button hidden there. I don't touch myself like this often. Only occasionally, but with clear pictures of Tyler in my head, I rub at my clit, my hips rising toward the attention. I explore, inserting one finger inside, slowly moving it in and out, then adding a second as thoughts of Tyler fill my mind. Tyler on top of me. Tyler shirtless, powerful. Tyler, intense and focused. I imagine wrapping my hand around his cock and guiding it inside me. What it would be like to have him fuck me.

God, yes...

I use my fingers as I writhe and cry out, coming at the thought of being with him. It's an orgasm that makes my feet tingle and my breath escape. When the aftershocks stop, I curl into a ball on my side, closing my eyes, wishing desperately that I did not want what I should not have.

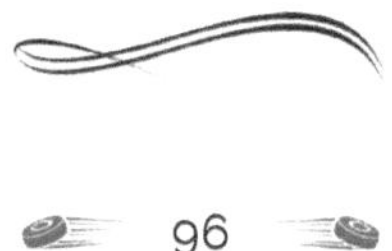

WHILE SHOWERING THE NEXT MORNING, I'm determined to put my mind off Tyler Lockhardt. It had to have been the alcohol that made me feel that way last night, right?

I wash my body, between my legs still sensitive from what I did the night before. I allow my fingers to linger there, reliving the sensation of coming with thoughts of Tyler in my head. But I quickly pull away. I have to focus. Study. That's what I'm here for.

I'M due to meet some friends, including my sister, for a study date at the local coffee shop. Jay is there when I arrive, his smile bright and wide as I walk in.

"Hey there," he says, shoving a frozen, green drink across the table at me. "Got you a green tea smoothie."

"Well, that was nice of you," I say, giving him a smile in return. "I owe you one next time."

He rubs his chin and looks down at his open biology notes, pleased with himself.

My sister joins in after about a half hour, bleary and looking terribly unkempt. Her hair is total bed head, her skin pale.

"Rough morning?" I ask as she plops into the seat next to me.

"I think I drank too much," she groans, putting her head on the table. "Fucking shots. Whose idea was that?"

"Yours, sister."

"Fuck my life."

"And fuck Tyler Lockhardt as well?" I *can't* stop myself from asking the question.

"Ugh. No. I was too drunk. Did he stop over to check on you like I asked?"

My cheeks go up in flames, I swear. I look away, pretending to dig in my bag, trying to get myself under control. "Yep, he did."

When I look back at her, she has an eyebrow raised in suspicion. "What happened between you two?"

"What? Nothing. What happened between the two of *you*? You were all over each other at the club."

"Wait," Jay interrupts. "Are you guys talking about the hockey player, Tyler Lockhardt, starting defenseman for the Crush?"

"Yes," Irina and I both answer at the same time.

"But...I thought you hated hockey players." Jay sounds slightly pathetic with a whiny, kid voice.

I give him a wan smile. "I do. But I got dragged with the two of them so Irina could get a tattoo, then we got dinner, then we went dancing. I left and those two were still going at it on the dance floor. Tyler swung by to make sure I got home okay. That was all."

"So nothing happened?" Irina presses, eager for more information.

"Of course not. Other than I decided he and I can be friends."

"Friends," my sister says flatly. "With a hockey player."

"I know, I know, I just think he needs someone to talk to, that's all." She raises an eyebrow at me in question. "If anything, I understand how often they are away or practicing."

"Who's Tyler Lockhardt?" Lily, one of our study friends asks.

"Mine," Irina answers Lily with a wicked grin on her face before googling him and showing his picture. Jay looks uncomfortable while the women all ogle the hot, shirtless pictures of Tyler the hockey star.

I peer closely, taking in the ink covering his upper body. A huge graffiti-like piece is on his chest, and several pieces work up his arms. It looks good on him, I admit, and thankfully my subtle drooling is overshadowed by the squeals of the other women at the table. Irina is saying how he is going to be her next conquest. How she's going to take that bad boy all the way to church. I can't help but laugh at the expression.

"He is a bad boy, I agree, but he has a good heart. Be kind to him, sister, or you will have his new BFF to contend with."

"I just want to fuck him, Zoya. It's not complicated and it won't break his heart. It might break other things, though..."

The women howl at this and I blush all the way to the tips of my ears. I go back to my studying, trying hard to focus only on the schoolwork in front of me. But in the back of my mind, thoughts of Tyler are there. Nagging feelings of jealousy and want. Feelings I don't want to admit I have.

"These idiots are annoying me," I finally say to Jay.

"Want to go somewhere else? I have stats in an hour and I really need to study."

He brightens. "I am not good at stats but yes, I would be happy to join you somewhere else, away from the Tyler Lockhardt mutual admiration club."

We gather our things and wander out into the bright sunlight. "The sun feels good. Want to sit outside?"

Jay says he is "game" for anything, which I guess means sitting outside will be okay. We find a grassy spot on campus and spread out, me with my confounding statistics homework in front of me, Jay with his biology flash cards and notes.

"Your sister is…" He stops, shaking his head.

"Direct? A slut?"

He chuckles. "She's something."

"Yes, she is. Irina is very much about shock value, half the time. Tyler is a conquest to her, so she can say she slept with a pro-athlete. My brother will probably go ballistic if he finds out."

"Your brother is protective?"

"Lately, yes. He never was before we came here. It's like my father inhabits his body now."

"Invasion of the body snatchers?"

"I don't know what that means."

"It's a movie…never mind. I get what you mean. Does it bother you? That your dad and brother are so protective?"

"No, not me so much. It irks Irina, which is why she acts out so much."

"So, are you allowed to date?" Jay asks. His cheeks turn pink, which I find endearing.

"I'm an adult. My father wants me to stay away from wild hockey players and the party scene, and since I don't want a hockey boyfriend anyway, I think I should be fine."

He sits back, looking satisfied. I can see that he wants to try to ask me out again. And I could see it, maybe. He's very cute. All-American with his curly brown hair and pretty blue eyes. He's nice and smart. Could he be my prince charming? Maybe.

Sadly, deep down I know different.

No matter how I try to envision myself with a guy like Jay, who has become a good friend over these past weeks, my thoughts are *already* invaded by dreams of a certain hockey bad boy that I shouldn't want at all.

16
shoulda known

Tyler

March

We've just checked in to our hotel in Boston after playing games in New York, New Jersey, and Philadelphia. I'm psyched for a hometown game. I even sent word to my old gym teacher, Mr. Gunnersen, and set him up with club seats so he could watch the game in style.

Now, the hard call. I dial my mom's number.

"Hi Tyler," she answers right away.

"Hey, Ma. How's it goin'?"

"It's been all right," she says casually. "Got the money you sent. Still waitin' on the welfare shysters to get their shit together, so it helps."

That's the closest I'll ever get to a thank you from her, so I'll take it. "Good. Glad it helped. Hey, I'm in Boston for a game, and I thought I could get you and the kids some tickets. You could come cheer me on."

"Ah, no, I don't have a car and I'm not loadin' the kids up on the bus."

"I can send a car, Ma. Don't worry about getting there and back."

"Yeah, but it ain't just the gettin' there, is it? They'll get there and want T-shirts and hot dogs and popcorn and it'll be a whole big mess that I can't afford."

"Ma," I say, exasperated. "I got it. I'll take care of all of it. Just come watch me play. The kids will like it and then we can all go out to dinner after. It'll be something special for them and they'll be able to say *that's my big brother out there*. Just come."

She's quiet for a second, then she sighs. "Okay. Fine, fine. We'll come."

"Awesome." I let out a sigh of relief. "I'll send a car at six and they'll drop you at Will Call. You'll go to the window and tell them your name and then they'll give you a packet of tickets, concession vouchers, T-shirts, and all that. Then after the game, just stay in your seats and I'll have someone bring you to me so we can go eat. Okay?"

"Fine, okay," she says.

"See you later then."

She hangs up without saying goodbye. Typical. At least the kids will be excited about seeing me play and get to have a fun night away from home.

I call Vik next and ask him to put Scarlett on the line, then explain what I need from her. She's been traveling with the team for long road trips like this one since she returned from maternity leave. They even bring a nanny and baby Alex on these trips. Somehow the three of them make it all work. Craziness indeed.

"I didn't know you had family here, Tyler," she says all excited. "That's so cool."

"Yeah, we'll see. I think my little brother and sister will like it, but my ma is weird about shit like this."

"Well, either way, I'll get everything ready for you down there."

"Thanks, Red, you're a lifesaver."

Viktor gets on the line after she says goodbye and gives me shit. "What is this about little brother and sister? I have no knowledge of these children."

"I don't talk about 'em," I explain. "Half-brother and -sister. They're real young. Four and six."

"This is new information, friend. I thought you were an orphan."

"Or demon spawn. Yeah, I got it. You're not the first."

"I can meet them?"

"We'll see, big guy. They can be a lot. I'll see ya later in the locker room."

I hang up, tense, and decide to head to the gym for a bit to blow off some steam. One of the trainers is in there and he helps me work through a light workout, so I don't end up hurting myself before the game. I want to call Zoya. I keep thinking about her.

Fuck it. I'm gonna call.

I finish the workout and head to grab my bag from the room, dialing Zoya's number as I swig some water.

"Hello, Tyler," she answers quickly as if she's actually happy to hear from me. As opposed to Ma who probably answers on the first ring in case she can get more outta me.

"Hey. Just wanted to check in on my favorite smokeshow before I go play."

"Boston?"

"Yeah..." I say, and it comes out a little shaky. "I invited my ma and the kids to come. I hope it doesn't turn into a shitshow."

"I'm sure it will be fine," she says in that sweet voice that surprisingly soothes me. "Play well. Call me later if you want to talk."

"I will. Call you, I mean. I assume you won't be watching?"

"I don't watch hockey if I can help it, but I will hope for a win."

"Okay. Thanks. Talk to you later."

We hang up and I shake out my arms, trying to rid myself of these weird jitters I have going on. This is just a game, like any other game, I try to convince myself.

It's no big thing.

Just another game.

THIS GAME IS HELLA TIGHT. Boston is out for blood and their right winger is on fucking fire. He's just shot after shot on goal, blasting the puck at us.

We can't do much but try to fend him off. He's a machine. And we knew it, because he's been playing like this all damn season, but for whatever reason, we weren't prepared for this tonight. Maybe we're tired after three other games on the road, but we have got to get our asses in gear. Boris and Mikhail and Evan need to push past their brick of a center defenseman and get some puck in net, like stat.

The buzzer goes off for the end of the second period and I'm drenched in sweat. I gulp down a shit-ton of Gatorade, pulling my gloves off and throwing them on the ground. Evan is yelping at everyone, *shut that guy down.* Yeah, no shit, Sherlock. That's all we've been doin' all damn game. If the guy was a motherfucking baseball player, he'd be swinging for the fences like it's the Home Run Derby. Fuck. Where did this kid come from?

Plus, they're physical as hell, which normally doesn't bother me, but I'm honestly tryin' not to get in a fight with my little brother and sister in the stands. My temper is hot, though, and one more check by their monstrous center forward and I will put that asshole's head in a vise and pop it off.

I breathe in, and blow out, several times, trying to center my brain. We're tied one-one heading into the third period. I'm sure as hell not goin' down without a fight.

We head back out, refocused, and about three minutes in, I see an opening to the Ice Dragon. I hang on to the puck long enough to fake like I'm going to pass it to Evan, but I wing it past him over to Boris, who chucks it right into the goal. Fuck yeah, an assist! Boris and I high-five, our ugly mugs up on the jumbotron for all to see.

Our second score of the period comes on a power play resulting from a big fight between that center and Mikhail. We're up a player and we use the advantage, Evan taking us to three-two just two minutes before the buzzer ends the game.

The Boston crowd is not happy, though there are a few chants for "Lockhardt" since it's known that I'm a Beantown native.

We do a few press snippets and then head to the locker room. I chuck my contacts, which are burning because of the sweating I'm doing, and head for a shower. Once I'm dressed and have found my glasses buried deep in my gym bag, I look at my phone, ready to call to meet up with Ma and the kids for dinner. I looked for them in the stands throughout the game, but it was impossible to pick them out in the crowd.

I wander out in the hallway, expecting to see familiar faces waiting, but they're nowhere to be found. What I do find is a stressed-out looking Scarlett, who grabs my arm and pulls me off, away from the crowd.

"What's up, Red? Did you find my family?"

She cringes.

"What?"

"Um…I don't really know how to tell you this—"

"Just spit it out. Are they okay?"

She lets out a shaky breath. "I went out to meet your mom at the gate, thought I'd get a little picture or something for social media, you know? Will Call told me she'd just been in and picked up the packet, so I walked outside, hoping to find her, and there was a big commotion on the street corner right in front of The Garden. Turns out, your mother tried to scalp the tickets, the vouchers and merch. The police came and they ended up searching her...and they—they found—d-drug paraphernalia..."

My stomach is on the floor. *What the actual fuck?*

"I guess it turned into an altercation, so they cuffed her and threw her in one cruiser, then loaded the kids into a second car." Scarlett is near to tears, now.

"Fuuuuck." It's all I can think to say.

"I'm so sorry, Tyler. I tried to get the cops to leave them all with me, but with the drugs...they said they had to arrest her. I didn't know what to do and I didn't want to mess up your game."

"It's not your fault, Red. This is why I don't talk to folks about my family. This is who my mother is." *How could she fucking do this?* "Do you... do you know what's going to happen to the kids?"

Scarlett is crying openly, now, obviously deeply affected by the whole scene she witnessed. *Been there, Red. Bought the T-shirt and everything.*

I pull her into a hug and remind her again and again that this isn't her fault. She has nothing to be sorry for. I thank her for keeping the whole fucked-up mess as discreet as possible before the start of the game.

Through sad tears, she tells me she just wants to go hold her baby.

I don't blame her.

Me? I don't think I've ever wanted to punch a hole in something more than I do at this moment.

I should have known.

I should have fucking known this would happen.

17
hit me with it

Zoya

Have I mentioned how much I hate statistics? Well, let me mention it again, because it frustrates me to no end. What will I ever do with this knowledge, please tell me.

My phone rings and I startle at the intrusion. It's nearly midnight so I know it must be Tyler, post-game.

"Hey there, BFF," I answer, happy to hear from him. "Did you win?"

"We did. Tight, tough game."

"Oh, good. But sorry it was a tough game. You sound tired."

"I'm fuckin' exhausted," he barks. Then quickly followed by, "I'm sorry. That wasn't nice and it wasn't directed at you."

"It's all right. Do you need to talk? How was your time with your family?"

"Ahhh..." I can hear frustration in his every word. "I didn't see them."

"Oh? Why not?"

"Because my fucking mother not only brought drugs to the game, but tried to hawk the tickets and merch I'd set aside for her and the kids. Right in front of the arena. In my hometown." I don't know Tyler very well, but the anger I can hear in his voice worries me.

"She tried to sell all the things you had for her and the kids? I'm so sorry." I know the words don't do much to help, but I want him to know I care.

He then launches into telling me that his mom was arrested for drug possession. He says Scarlett, his teammate's wife, tried to help, and now she's really upset. "I just feel sick, ya know?"

"Yeah. I'm not surprised," I say sadly.

"And the worst thing, Zoya, is that my little brother and sister had to see that shit. They had to watch her get in an altercation with the cops, then they got loaded up in a cop car and taken to who the hell knows where. It's so fuckin' frustrating. I had this fun night planned for them and then she goes and shits on it. Every time, Zoya. Every fucking time."

"I am so sorry, Tyler." My heart just breaks for him.

"I should've known she was lying about being better. I should've known she'd make this about money, or making money, or whatever. And now I'm really worried about Haley and Logan. They're little, Zo. They shouldn't be around this shit."

"Maybe you could go to the police station and tell them you are their brother. Maybe the kids could come to the hotel with you for at least the night while things get sorted out? Is there someone you can call to help you with it?"

Tyler is quiet for a long time. "You know, I think I will call my lawyer and see what he can arrange. Thanks."

"No problem. That's what friends are for."

"Yeah, okay, *buddy*," he says. I can hear humor in his voice like he's trying hard to shake off the awfulness of his night. I suppose I already know that friendship isn't all he wants from me. And I'm stressing about it because I need to hold him at arm's length. I cannot fall for him. It's not what I want in the long-term. "What are you doing? Sorry, I shit on you with all my problems tonight," he says sadly.

"It's okay. Your problem is much more important than mine."

"Which is?"

"Statistics. I hate it."

"Well, Smokeshow, it's your lucky night. I'm damn good at stats, thank you very much. Read me the problem you're workin' on."

"Really?"

"Yeah, really. It'll help me calm down from all this bullshit for a minute. Hit me with it."

I read the problem, and he talks me through every step. The way he explains it makes so much more sense than what I read in the book. We finish one problem, then do a few more. After an hour, my assignment is done, and I feel ten times lighter.

"I need you every day to help me with this stuff. Oh my God, thank you so much."

"Does it make more sense now?"

"Yes. My father told me I could get a tutor, and now I see how having someone who knows this can help me, I might just do that."

He scoffs on the other end of the line. "Why would you pay a tutor when you could just ask me?"

"Well, you *are* busy playing hockey you know."

"Never too busy for my BFF. You need help and I'm gonna give it to you. Fun fact—I worked under the table for a sports bookie when I was a kid. I got really good at doing the stats."

"Well, I guess you should put that power to a good purpose, then."

"What's in it for me, Zo?"

"My undying friendship and loyalty." As soon as the words are out of my mouth, I realize I'm not feeling them with any sort of conviction anymore because *I wish I could tell him it was more.*

He blows a raspberry. "Blah. Okay, I mean, I guess if that's all..."

"It's all." *For now.*

"Anything for you, Smokeshow. Thanks for the talk. And the idea. I gotta go take care of this shit now. Call you tomorrow with an update."

He seems marginally happier when we hang up and it makes me feel good to know I helped him, even if only a little. Still, I worry about him and his family and what he has to do now to try and make things better for his young siblings. God, so *very young.* His head must be spinning. And I feel so useless, especially given he is literally on the other side of the country and I can do nothing to help. I have nothing to offer him, and that brings stress to my heart.

It also makes me wonder just how Tyler Lockhardt got past my defenses and into my heart so quickly.

Because you know that he has.

18
in the f#cking world

Tyler

I pace the floor of my hotel room and stress the fuck out. Could I really go down to the station and pick up my little brother and sister, just like that? And if I did, what would I do with them? I'm supposed to head back to Vegas tomorrow.

The alternative, I suppose, is that they get put into children's protective services or split up in some shitty foster home somewhere. I can't stomach that. No way.

But Ma is right about one thing. I'm barely a functioning adult myself. I can't take care of two little kids, can I? The idea of it is totally crazy. Still, they're my brother and sister, my blood. The only blood family I have. And they're so small. *Fuck this world.* I don't want them growing up in some dump with filth and drugs and predators all around. I want them to have good lives and futures, far, far the fuck away from the shitshow life they've been trapped in. I want them to get out like I did.

I call my attorney, Jack Engelland, and explain my situation.

"I know your job is to handle, like, contracts and shit, but I don't know who else to call, Jack. I'm backed against a brick wall here." I'm not opposed to begging after telling him the whole, crazy fucked-up story. "I can't just leave the kids to the system, not when they have me—I mean, I'm their brother and I have the means to take care of them. At least until we find a better solution."

"No problem, man," Jack reassures me. He's a fairly young guy. I've even partied with him. He knows me and he knows when I'm being serious. "I'll make some calls. Figure out what's going on and report back with options. I do know someone who can at least give you the basics. She's a social worker in Boston, and the wife of one of my law school buddies. Her name's Winter Blakney and she'll know how to get the ball rolling."

"Thanks, man. Sorry for calling you in the middle of the damn night."

"No worries. Call you as soon as I get some intel."

We hang up and I pace the room like a caged animal. I have so much unspent energy, so much anger and worry and frustration. See, this is why I compartmentalize my life the way I do. I keep my mom and her bullshit in a separate box. I've spent ninety percent of my life fucking around, because fucking around is a helluva lot better than feeling the way I feel right now.

I consider going out. There are probably after

parties happening around town. I could find a nice, little puck bunny to stick my dick into. Let off some steam. Get a release. I should've been out partying with my teammates tonight. We fought for that win. We pulled it out. But damn, now I'm here in my hotel, sick with worry for two kids that I hardly even know.

I should've been more involved. Maybe I should've tried harder, moved them out to Vegas with me, Ma included. She hasn't been right for a long time. I guess I just felt that staying away and staying out of their lives for the most part was the best way to keep the stress and anxiety at bay. I always felt like even though my mom was making shitty choices, the kids were still okay. Getting what they needed, but that's not the case. They're neglected and possibly suffering abuse.

And the guilt overtakes me like a toxic cloud seeping into every crack and fissure of vulnerability I own.

You play a game with a stick, son. Anyone could do that.

You're lucky they took a chance on you, son. You wouldn't have amounted to much more than that anyway.

Glad you left when you did. I didn't need another mouth to feed, son. 'Specially a useless one like you.

Was she like that with the kids now? Fuck. I'd been kidding myself. If the first chance to take my siblings to one of my matches ended with her hawking shit for cash, then Haley and Logan have always been in harm's way. *And I've been oblivious.*

Have run as far away as I could so I wouldn't have to see it firsthand.

I left before they were born. I barely acknowledged they existed at first. I mean, shit, I was a freshman in college when Haley was born. A junior when Logan came along. Ma was young when she had me, like eighteen. She was in her mid-thirties when she had another baby, with a guy she said was good, who would stick around. I can only guess if he's Logan's dad, too, but he beat feet soon after the little guy was born, and Ma went way downhill after that. I just couldn't deal with it. I had pro teams looking at me, a chance to make something of myself with the only thing that ever made any sense in my life.

I think about calling Zoya again. I want to call Zoya again. Because she…*listens.* No one has ever really listened to me. But then again, have I ever really had anything to say? *Hookups. Drunken parties.* No. I can't bug her with this shit. I mean, she calls herself my BFF, but I think she just says it to make sure I know the boundaries. Friend zone, only.

I make myself lie down on the couch, falling into one of those fitful sleeps that doesn't ever feel like real sleep at all. Because it isn't.

Straight-up fuckin' dream warfare.

WHEN MY PHONE RINGS AGAIN, I sit bolt upright, my heart about to lunge out of my chest. It's Jack, and it's nine in the morning.

"Okay, I located the kids. Children's services interviewed them. I guess they spent the night in a holding cell, which has got to be goddamn terrifying, and I gave them an earful about it, believe me."

"But they're okay?"

"Far as I can tell. The report indicates they were supposed to watch their brother play hockey when their mother decided to sell the tickets, so there is confirmation from them that you're their sibling. The person from children's services says your mom will be held until her initial hearing. They think she'll have several charges to contend with, possession of methamphetamine, child endangerment times two, a fraud charge, and a charge for assaulting an officer. It doesn't look good for her, probably at least eighteen months in jail. So, I asked for emergency, temporary custody for you until we can get a lay of the land and figure out a longer-term solution that works for everyone."

It hits me like a ton of bricks. Temporary custody. Of two small children. Holy fuuuuck. *Is this the right thing? Should I be doing this?*

"Yo, Tyler, you still with me?" Jack's voice penetrates through the shock. "This is what you want, right? They said they can put the kids into foster care, but it's always better if a family member can take them in. I figured that was what you wanted."

"Yeah," I breathe. "Yep. Yes. That's what I want. Tell me what's next."

"I got a hold of Winter, the social worker I told you about, and she's now the case manager of record.

I've texted you her info. She'll bring the kids over to the hotel, interview you, talk about options and next steps with you. I can call you back if it gets into a legal conversation. I'll stay at the ready."

"Thanks, Jack, you're saving my life right now."

"I've got you. But do have the conversation with Brown and Bellikowski as soon as you can. You'll have to stay in Boston for a while to get this sorted. Get team management up to speed with what's going on with you. Family takes precedence over sports. Remember that. We're not living in the dark ages anymore. They'll support you through this so don't worry about that part, but do let me know if you need me to intervene. Talk to you soon."

"I'M GIVING you two weeks to get back on the ice, Lockhardt," Coach says on the other end of the line. "This family matter is a good thing you're doing, but we need you back here, too."

"I got ya, Coach. I want to be out on the ice with the guys as well."

"Make sure you check in with Dale on your daily workouts, so you stay in game shape. No snacking on donuts out there, son. Keep it tight and keep us in the loop, please."

Chuckling, I promise Coach to work out daily and "keep it tight" as he said. I thank him again for the time off. After I hang up, I find myself rubbing absently at an ache pounding away in my chest.

Heartburn, maybe? This shit is stressful. Two emotionally packed phone calls have my head good and spinning. I need a shower. I need to put on something other than a T-shirt and workout shorts. The kids might be hungry. I'm hungry.

After ordering a ton of room service, I take a quick shower and throw on a nice shirt and some jeans. The food comes, and just a few minutes later, there's another knock at the door.

A drop-dead gorgeous woman with long dark hair and a medium-sized baby bump stands there with Logan and Haley, one in each hand. Not at all what I'd expect a social worker in Southie to look like, but what the fuck do I know about anything right now. She's brought them here and they're safe.

"Tyler Lockhardt?"

"That's me."

"Nice to meet you. I'm Winter Blakney and I have two sweeties here who really want to see you." The kids both look scared and tired as they hold on to her, their little faces so small and innocent that I can't help but crouch down to their level. They instantly step forward and I pull them into a tight hug.

"You guys okay?" I whisper.

Both of their heads bob up and down.

"We got arrested!" Haley exclaims.

"Did they put the cuffs on ya?" I ask, trying to keep it light.

"They put us in the back of a police car," she says, wide-eyed.

"Well, let's go inside. I have breakfast for you."

"Hungry!" Logan yelps, bounding inside.

I invite Winter in, and we sit on the couch, the array of food on the coffee table in front of us. After helping the kids fill their plates, they dive in like they haven't been fed in days. For sure nothing as tasty and as healthy as this spread. It makes me feel fuckin' sad. It also makes me realize something... I *am* doing the right thing. Even if this is terrifying for me, it's nothin' to what's been going on for these two little guys.

I tell Winter to help herself to anything she'd like, and she opts for some herbal tea and a muffin. Pregnant women need food regularly throughout the day, right? I don't want to be a burden to her straight off the bat, but I'm guessing she only took on this case as a favor to Jack. And I'm pretty fuckin' sure being woken up in the middle of the night wasn't on a pregnant lady's list of shit to do today.

"Thank you. I just want you to know how much I appreciate your help, Winter. I don't know where to really even start with this and Jack said he knew you so..." My words sort of peter out, pathetically, exactly like I feel right now.

"No worries, Tyler. This is my job and I love doing it. Helping families through tough times is what it's all about, you know?"

I nod slowly a few times, unsure of what to even say. Right now, I figure it's best for me to just listen to her and learn everything I can.

"So, the purpose of my visit is to assess the best course of action to take in the temporary placement of Haley and Logan during the absence of your mother.

I'm here to talk to you and get a feel for your relationship with Haley and Logan and find out what your wishes are. I'll have to make a recommendation to the court, so this is the first step in that process."

"Got it." I nod again, the limit of my ability to react intelligently, apparently. Fuck.

She smiles gently and takes a sip of her tea before reaching over to help Logan put some strawberry jam on an English muffin. Then she shows him how to use the napkin to wipe the sticky off his hands.

I almost have to blink back the tears that threaten to bust out of my eyes. The kids don't even know the basic manners of how to eat a goddamn meal. Jesus.

"So, Tyler...the kids have shared some pretty concerning stuff with us since we brought them in last night." She says this without judgment, but I still feel the heavy weight of it settling over me.

"I'm not sure I want to hear the details, but I doubt it's much different than what I experienced growing up."

"Multiple men in and out of the house. Drug use, though they don't understand that's what they're seeing. Some instances of physical abuse and neglect. Often being left alone for hours on end, not knowing where Mom is. It's been very scary for them."

Hot shame and guilt fill every cell in my body. *No different than what my youth was like*, and it makes me feel like the worst person ever that I didn't step in, didn't do more to get them out of the shitshow life they're trapped in.

Winter, who's probably seen this sort of thing

countless times, correctly reads my body language. "Hey, none of this is your fault, you know. You didn't cause the situation."

"I don't know about that," I say, rubbing my hands over my face. I'm fucking exhausted, emotionally drained, and just feel like screaming to let out some of the tension. "I could've stepped in a long time ago, I suppose. I kept trying… got them a place to live but she trashed it. Bought her a car, but she sold it. Everything I did, I thought I was helping, and she always told me things were better and I wanted to believe her."

"It sounds like you did more than most people might," Winter says softly. "So, the focus now is getting the kids into a stable environment. They need somewhere calm and consistent. You're a professional hockey player. And before I go any further, I have to give you this disclosure. When I tell you I'm huge into hockey, you can believe me. I've followed the Crush and knew who you were long before today. My husband and I even met Georg and Pam Kolochev on our honeymoon. We were at the same island with them and so...yeah, I already know who you are just from following the team and being friends with Georg and Pam. Probably more than I *should* know about you if I'm being completely honest."

"Yeah." I know where this is going. "I do travel a lot, but I feel like I can figure this out. At least for the time being. I've got a nice place in Vegas with a bedroom already set up for them. I eat healthy. There are good schools in the area. I can hire someone to stay with them when I'm on the road. I'll do a background check, whatever."

"That all sounds great, but I can't see just putting them on a plane today, Tyler. There are some legal hoops, some vetting, that we need to do."

"Yeah, I get that I guess…it's just that I have a job back there, you know? I don't live here anymore. I can't stay here indefinitely."

"I know, and I think it will all be fine. What you're offering is better than most of the alternatives. Even if it's just for a few weeks or months while we find something more permanent. Or until your mother earns them back."

"I can't—I don't see that happening. She gets clean for short spurts but never for long. Never permanently."

"I have to confess, I googled you and had a look at what popped up…"

"And you found a bunch of pictures all over social media of me and women and booze?"

"Yep." She grins at me but it's not in a mean way, thankfully. Winter Blakney has got to be the coolest social worker in the whole fucking world. "You might want to tone that down going forward though."

"Done. The kids are more important right now."

Winter sucks her lips in and considers this—me— for a long moment. It unnerves me but I don't flinch away from the scrutiny. She's doing her job; she has to make a decision about me to recommend to the court. I get it.

"I'm happy to hear it, Tyler, but here's another

question for you. How is a twenty-four... five—twenty-something hockey player supposed to upend his life for two kids?"

"I'll work it out. I don't pretend to have all the answers about how I'll work it out, but I know I'll get there. Lots of the guys on my team have kids now. They learn how to be parents and play pro-hockey at the same time. Why can't I?"

"Do you have a partner or spouse?"

"No, but I have friends. I have teammates who can give me advice and recommendations. I have a university education and a brain too, in spite of appearances. I'm financially stable. I set up trust funds for the kids that no one even knows about so they can go to college one day. I invest well and I don't overspend. I can figure this out. I am *committed* to figuring it out."

"Okay, that's good. Any questions for me?"

I'm blank—*fuck, what should I be asking?* I look at Haley and Logan, who have sat quietly and eaten as we've spoken. I imagine this isn't how they always behave, but what the hell do I know? Fucking nothing.

"Um, what grade is Haley in? I feel so stupid asking that, Winter, but I haven't stayed close. Are they okay? Did a doctor check them? Do they sleep in beds? I used to sleep on a mattress on the floor for a while, so I don't even know if Ma gave them beds..."

As I hear Winter's gasp, my head snaps up to her.

"We'll find out all of those things, okay? My heart just broke about your bed when you were small. Or lack thereof. We need to go to their home and investigate more. Then we can grab clothes and toys while we're there. And just so you know, you're saying all of the right things. Good job, you."

I let out a sigh of relief so long and loud she laughs at me. At what must look like one shell-shocked dude in so far over his dumb, fucking, head, he's underwater. But her laughter is kind, so I don't mind a bit.

"So, here's the gig. I need you to stay in Boston for a few days. James, my husband, will get an emergency custody hearing set up and you'll say everything you told me to the judge. If he agrees, which I think he will, then we'll get dispensation for you to take them out of the state, at least temporarily. Then you can take them home with you to Vegas."

"Okay. I've already spoken to my coach. He's going to frontload the rest of the coaching staff and our GM. I've been granted two weeks family leave to get the kids settled with me in Vegas. I'll do whatever I need to do to make this work. Whatever it takes."

"You're saying all of the magic words I needed to hear from you, Tyler." Winter knocks me out with her million-dollar smile again and I know I hit the motherfucking lottery with her being our case manager. Small world though that she knows Georg and Pam. What are the chances of that? And bonus she's a hockey fan, because I doubt someone older and more jaded would've given me chance to help the kids.

"I'm so grateful for your help, Winter. Thank you,

thank you, thank you...for this. I won't let them down." I wanna hug her I'm so grateful, but I don't. Not a moron.

"I don't believe you will, Tyler Lockhardt. I'm an excellent judge of character, and I know a good heart when I feel one." She taps fingers over her heart and gives me a nod.

"You know, you and the hubs will have box seats for any game we're ever playin' at The Garden, right? I gotchu."

"And I'm sure this hockey fan will take you up on that offer whenever we can." She claps her hands together silently. "Did I tell you my favorite saying, Tyler?"

"You did not."

"Either you like hockey or you're wrong."

So. Fucking. Lucky.

19
wacko

Zoya

"How's your vegan pasta?" Georg asks Irina from across the table, before sticking his finger down his throat and making a gagging noise.

My sister rolls her eyes and gives him the finger. "I don't know. How's the dead carcass of whatever animal gave its life without consent? Does it taste like murder?"

"If it does," Georg answers while shoving a big piece of steak into his mouth, "then my favorite meal is murder."

"You are a pig." Irina glares at him. "*Ti degeheneraat.*"

"Okay, okay." Georg smirks at her in delight. "Simmer down, little sister."

Pam diffuses the situation. "Tell me about your thesis, Irina."

"Well, I am toying with the idea of investigating the issue of voluntary human trafficking."

"Just a light topic," I mutter as Irina elbows me.

"It's just that I have been hearing about women and children in low-income communities who perform work or sex acts for money or drugs or shelter and they do it because they truly believe they're helping their families. I want to investigate that, in order to better understand both poverty and the differences in how people define human trafficking."

"Wow," Pam says, sounding impressed. "I just stretch people out after they get injured."

Irina lifts a shoulder and stabs at her pasta. "I plan to go for my PhD and then teach. I think it's important to not be afraid of difficult topics in research."

"It sounds like a really interesting project," Pam says. "I think you'll learn a lot by looking at the family dynamics in the case studies. I'll bet you could take the research in many different directions."

"Yes, right," Irina says, nodding. "I'm actually having a hard time narrowing the focus right now. My advisor is stressing that I need to follow one string, not the whole web."

"Good advice," Pam says.

"Speaking of webs," Georg says. "Pam, did you hear this insanity about Tyler Lockhardt? They gave him a four-game leave of absence. Said he had some family matters to attend to but didn't tell us what. I didn't realize he even had a family. I thought he might have been raised by wolves."

"I know," Pam says. "I mean, I know he's out on leave. Not the wolves part."

"He's working on getting emergency custody of his little brother and sister," I say, finally happy to be able to contribute something to the conversation."

"His what?" Georg asks. "He has siblings?"

"A four-year-old half-brother and a six-year-old half-sister," I say, nodding. "His mother was arrested trying to hawk the tickets he got for them in Boston. She ended up getting many charges filed against her and the kids were going to have to go into protective services, so Tyler is getting emergency custody so he can bring them back to Vegas."

Irina's eyes are wide. "You didn't tell me any of that."

I shrug and give her a sideways glance before shoving a piece of chicken in my mouth. When I look up at Georg, he's glaring at me.

"How do you know all of this?" he asks.

"Oh, Zoya and Tyler are best friends now, Georg," Irina chirps. "Didn't you know? They talk all the time."

I kick my sister under the table. Hard.

"*Sluha vokzal'naja,*" my sister hisses.

"*Moodozvon,*" I snarl in return.

Pam's brow furrows as she says, "I thought I was getting all the Russian swears down, but those two are new to me."

"It's okay, baby," Georg answers. "I will translate. Irina called Zoya a *train station whore* and Zoya responded with the not-nearly-as-creative *wacko.*"

"Ahh," Pam says. "Well then, I agree, Zoya, you need to up your insult game."

We all giggle at this, but Georg is soon right back on topic. "Seriously, you're not supposed to be hanging with hockey players, Zoya. Strict orders from the motherland. Or fatherland, to be more accurate. Plus, you hate everything hockey. How could you possibly want to hang around someone who is as stereotypically hockey as Tyler Lockhardt?"

"He needed a friend."

"But don't you think they must be getting *very close* if he told her about his family and no one else?" Irina prods. "I am sure Papa would not approve."

"Well, I'm not the one fucking him," I blurt before slapping my hand over my mouth, eyes wide.

Pam swallows a grin by pretending to cough into her napkin. Irina returns the under-table kick.

"I'm sorry?" Georg asks. "What did you just say?"

I push my lips together and look down at the table.

He points his index finger at me. "I'll deal with Irina in a minute. What kind of language is that out of a young woman?"

"Don't be a hypocrite." Pam snorts. "She's an adult and she can use whatever language pleases her. And besides, it's not like you or I don't say the word fuck every seven seconds."

"Not the fucking point," Georg argues.

"Well, then, what is the point?" Pam asks, folding her arms over her chest. "Because it sounded like you were scolding a nineteen-year-old woman for saying a curse word so pervasive that it barely has meaning anymore."

"Oh, Christ," Georg groans, throwing his head back. "Whatever. What. Ever. Fine, Zoya, say fuck all you want. But Irina, is this true? Are you sleeping with him? Because he is the worst kind of slut out there. He is not good for you. He doesn't care about women at all. He thinks they're just playthings. He drinks too much. Can't keep his mouth shut. Can't keep his temper in check. Papa will have an aneurysm if he finds out. He'll probably ship you two right back to Russia."

"Georg Kolochev," Irina snaps. "I am twenty-two and able to make my own decisions, especially when it comes to my own body and my own sex life. And if you must know, I haven't really talked to him since the night I got my tattoo."

I snicker beside her, *because...*

"What?!" Georg explodes. "Your what? I think I heard you say tattoo, but that can't really be what you said."

"Yes, I got a tattoo. I like tattoos. And it's beautiful and meaningful and I will probably get more at some point. Chill out. It's my body."

I think Georg's teeth might crack; he's gritting them so hard.

"What the hell is happening here?" Georg is really laying the guilt on thick.

"Calm down please," Pam says softly, leaning toward him, her fingers brushing at the back of his neck. "You're going to make a scene."

Georg snorts and shakes his head.

"They're adults, Georg. They can make their own decisions and choices. They came here to have some freedom. Plus, maybe it's good for someone like Tyler to have girls like these as friends. They're smart and capable and they don't take any bullshit. He can learn how to be friends with a woman, how to respect a woman and value her opinion."

"I was given an explicit task—"

"I know, by your father," Pam states. "But you weren't so different from Tyler not too long ago yourself, and yet I still love you. And you love me. We're both proof that people can grow and change. And Zoya's already said she doesn't want to date a hockey player anyway, so what's the harm in them having a friendship?"

"Thanks," I say to Pam and she winks back at me.

"But why are you friends with *him*?" Georg whines. "He's such an asshole."

I laugh a little. "I thought so too, at first. Then I realized he's just acting out to forget... Tyler has had a much harder life than he has shared, and he needed someone to talk to about that."

"Why can't he just go see a shrink like a normal person?"

"I don't think he realized he needed to talk about it until...well, until he started talking about it. But he needs it, he really does, and I don't want to be another person who lets him down. I will not stop being his friend."

Georg stares a hole in me until finally sighing

deeply. "Fine. Okay. I trust you to not let things go too far with him. I'm going to *trust* you, Zoya."

"Just her?" Irina asks.

"You don't want to be his *friend*," Georg says pointedly.

"So?"

"So, he probably has like forty diseases."

"To be fair, how many women did *you* sleep with before you settled down with Pam?" Irina asks. "Do you have forty diseases?"

"He does not," Pam says. "We both got tested before we got married."

"I'm just saying that Georg's picture was all over the Internet for a long time, with many different women," Irina explains. "It's one of the reasons our father *didn't* let us come to America."

"That's true, Georg," I add.

Georg raises his hands. "I don't know. People change. I changed. I fell in love. I stopped drinking. It was a life choice and I'm glad I made it."

I say, "So if you can change—"

"Then Tyler can, too," Irina finishes.

"And you think that you're going to be the one to settle him down, Irina?" Georg asks. "You are his Pam?"

Irina lets out a howl of laughter. "Hell no, I just want to have sex with him."

My sister's words hit me right in the heart. It feels like...jealousy. And even though I know I shouldn't be jealous of anyone who wants to have sex with Tyler, I am. *I totally am.*

"No," Georg says, shaking his head furiously. "No way."

"You're acting like a dad," Irina says.

Georg grits his teeth again. "Fine. I don't want to be anybody's damn dad. Whatever. Do what you want. Go fuck manwhore hockey players if you want to. You're right, it's your body. It's your life. But I'm telling our father that I told you all the reasons this would be a bad idea. I'm not taking the blame for this disaster."

"Okaaay," Irina says, rolling her eyes. "Thanks for the blessing to go out and get laid, then. *Zasranec.*"

Georg gets out his wallet to pay the bill, muttering something about assholes.

We leave, Pam inviting us back to their apartment to play board games. I think it's her attempt at an olive branch. She wants to make peace between us and Georg, which is really sweet. I also appreciate how she stood up for us at the table. Pam is good—as golden to us as she is to Georg. Thankfully, my brother did see Pam for the amazing woman she is. I'm not sure if it was in the process of scooping her up that he became a better man, or if he was simply... ready. Ready to be the changed man. The family man. Like Papa.

I still have no clue what will happen with Tyler with his new charges. Will it change his ways? He's never had a family worth emulating before, unlike Georg. *Does it matter, Zoya? You'll never be his Pam... just his friend.* There will probably still be many women like Irina in his life. And I have to be happy with that, as it was the wisest thing for me. For my heart.

"BANANAS!" I yell, holding up my hands.

"Damn it!" Irina yells, placing her last tiles on Bananagrams just a moment after I yell out the winning word. "Word nerd strikes again."

"You're so good at this game," Pam says. "Extra points since English isn't your first language."

"This game actually helped me with my English," I say. "My tutor in Russia always used it because it required me to think on my feet."

"She mops the floor with us every time we play," Georg says, looking sheepishly at his paltry crossword, many of his tiles still not placed in words.

"I have always been good at word-related things," I say. "Math and statistics, though? Ugh."

"Still having trouble with that class?" Irina asks. "Papa said you could get a tutor."

"I was trying to figure it out on my own, but the other night, Tyler helped me over the phone. I think he will keep helping me."

Georg, who has wandered off to sit on the couch, turns around to look at us. "Just how close are the two of you, anyway?"

"Go back to your sports highlights, brother," I tell him, annoyed.

Irina giggles. "I love that this is bothering you so much, Georg."

"Why?" His tone is funny, whiny, perplexed.

"Because you spent a long time not worrying about anyone or having any responsibility and now, you're getting hit hard by it. Payback is a cruel bitch, true?" Irina has always been one to taunt. It was actually very quiet for me when she was living away at university and I was the only one at home. She hasn't changed, and I cannot say I missed her sharp tongue.

I think they're finding it amusing to see you adulting, honey," Pam adds.

"Adulting is hard," Georg whines, flopping back on the couch. "I feel really uncomfortable about this... this—"

"Friendship," I say. "It is a friendship, *dodogoy brat.*"

"Ugh," he grunts. "Whatever. I don't have to like it, *dear* sister."

I make a face at him. "He's a good guy underneath. Cocky on the outside, softer on the inside. He needs a friend and I want to be there for him."

Georg just sighs and waves me off, done with the serious-ish conversations for the night. He turns on ESPN and ignores us while we set up for another round of the game. As I flip my tiles, I look over at Pam and find myself blushing under the knowing weight of her stare.

My sister-in-law knows there is a lot more to this story.

I even think she knows there are things I'm not saying...about Tyler Lockhardt.

20
how's it possible?

Tyler

Ten days later.

There's been court dates and interviews. And because Haley and Logan came to me literally with the clothes on their backs and nothing more, shopping trips to places like Target and Kohl's. Basically, it's been a crash course in kidlet for the three of us this past week. They don't have experience or knowledge in what kids need any more than I do. They've been living in conditions far worse than anything I ever experienced as a kid.

Back to the guilt tripping later.

Winter has been a godsend. She set me up with an intern from children's services who helped me shop online for the myriad of things the kids will possibly need for school and normal daily life. I literally had no clue what that entailed. Pretty much everything is the short answer. Oh, stuff like age-appropriate clothing that fits and isn't dirty or ripped. Ditto for shoes, pajamas, coats, backpacks, kid toothbrushes, plus a few items they chose for themselves like blankets and toys and books. Thank you, Amazon Prime.

I was close to tears watching Haley choose a quilt set with unicorns for herself and dinosaurs for Logan, especially when she asked if she would really get her own bed and not have to share with her brother? And why? Because she'd have more room? Because she was too big to share a bed with her brother? No. Nothing so normal as any of those reasons. It was because her sheets were often wet when she'd forgotten to change Logan's diaper before bedtime when Ma wasn't there. Apparently, he wasn't potty trained overnight. And sometimes, she hadn't done laundry, so there were no sheets to replace the soiled ones.

Fuckin' six-years-old and changin' her little brother's diaper... because her mom was out who knows fucking where. I'd never known such grief. Anger.

My cleaning lady, Marlena, has been unpacking everything Amazon has shipped, getting their room set up. I had Vik grab some guys to set up the beds. I also gave Marlena a raise and explained she'll be earning every cent of it. She's been an angel to do this for me, and I am just so appreciative of the help I've been given so far, not just from her, but a lot of people.

That said, it's still been a rough week for them. Haley and Logan have had to go see physicians and counselors and go to court to talk to the judge. It's been a whole clusterfuck simply tryin' to get temporary custody of my brother and sister. And I'm no dad, you know. I don't know what the hell I'm doing.

The judge sat up on his high horse while I was in there for the hearing. He was like, "Son, I see that you're a professional athlete. It's dubious you can play professional hockey and take care of two small children."

Winter's attorney husband, James Blakney, walked me through everything with the judge in Boston. Cool dude who loves hockey and his wife. I'm keeping my promise to treat them to seats whenever the Crush comes to Beantown. The very least I can do after all they've done to help me.

James had the forethought to get letters from Coach Brown, Crush owner Max Terry, and team captain, Evan Kazmeirowicz, all of them gushing about how committed I am to the team, how hardworking and responsible. It's all bullshit, I think, but I appreciate that they'd fib to make me look good. What I really think sold the whole thing is the many comments they made about how the whole organization would be committed to giving me as much support as needed to assure the kids would be safe and secure.

That part choked me up, I gotta admit.

A little tug at my sleeve and I'm looking down at a tiny, wide-eyed face. Logan's face. Honestly, he looks a little like I did as a kid, with blond hair and an impish grin. Haley's got darker hair, curly. She's more serious, I've realized. The caretaker, I think. She's protective of her little brother. I've spent countless hours feeling the shame of guilt that I haven't been there for them as I should've been. But that's for a shrink appointment on another day.

Right now, I gotta get two kids—who've never been on a plane before—on a flight to Las Vegas. They keep wandering off, wanting snacks, having to pee. It's a whole thing, managing these two in a place as busy as Boston-Logan. And holy hell, can I take a little girl into a dirty men's room in a packed airport? *Fuck, no is that answer.* But I can't let her go in the ladies' room by herself, either. Can I?

I am so not prepared for this.

We get some overpriced snacks and then make it to our gate where I could literally kiss the woman who lets us board early. The kids are excited to walk on the jet bridge, then onto the plane. Everything is a new experience for them, so I explain and explain to help them process it all. We've got first-class seats, so we sit right up front. One of the pilots greets the kids and even allows them to glance in at the cockpit before the door is closed. The flight attendant pins tiny wings on their shirts from the captain.

It's pretty cute, actually, how excited they are to fly. I think I've done it so many times that the shine has worn off, but I do remember my first flight. I wonder if they'll remember this one.

Once we reach altitude, I turn on a movie for them and they sit happily munching on treats. I keep hoping they'll pass out and take a nap, but they never do. We watch movies, get up to check out the bathroom, and order about fifteen different snacks and juice boxes and whatnot. Every time they're quiet and calm, I sit across the aisle from them, knees bouncing up and down and out of control, trying to imagine how the hell I'm going to do this. Be a parental type. I'm sure I'll be shit at it.

As we're making our final descent, I have the kids look out the window to see how different the terrain looks here than back home. Once we land it hits me like a ton of bricks...again. *I am now the legal guardian to two small children. Kids, welcome to Vegas.* Pushing down my momentary panic, I lead them off the plane and into McCarren International, the very first stop for them on their way to a brand-new life. *One baby step at a time, dude.* Thank you to whoever thought of family bathrooms though, because it means I can just take them together into one room and not have to deal with strangers. That brilliant concept deserves a fuckin' Nobel Prize or something.

We head down to baggage claim, where I see a man in a suit holding up a sign with "Lockhardt" on it. I'm thrilled about the driver, but it's his companion who really makes me smile. I can't believe it, but it's true. *Smokeshow came to the airport to meet us.*

"Zoya?"

She gives a radiant smile, heading toward me. Do I hug her?

Oh, yep. She's coming in for a hug. Wow. She smells amazing.

"Hey," I say as we pull apart. "What are you doing here?"

"I thought you might like to see a friendly face."

There's that friend word again. Always with the friend zone. Still, as she bends down and says, "Hi, I'm Zoya," and shakes the kids' hands, I'm choking up —again—because she bothered to come and meet us. I need to turn away to swallow it back before facing her again.

"This is Logan, and this is Haley." I touch each kid on the head as I introduce them.

"You two are so cute," Zoya says, crouching down to their level.

"She's *pretty*," Haley says as she looks up at me, wide-eyed.

I nod because Zoya *is* pretty. More than pretty. She is a feast, with her brown hair long and wavy, her lips plump, and her eyes dark and sultry. She doesn't try to be flashy or sexy. She's in jeans and a simple, gray T-shirt, her toes painted baby pink, on feet in simple black, leather flip-flops. But still, she takes my breath away and I don't know how to feel about that. I've seen plenty of beautiful women. I've slept with beautiful women. The difference? Zoya is unassuming. She's smart and quiet and steady. She's not falling all over herself to get my attention. And she listens. Really listens. Cares about the Tyler who grew up poor in Boston. The Tyler who just wanted to get away from his shitty life. The Tyler who's trying to get custody of his siblings to keep them from ending up somewhere awful.

I'm staring, made obvious by the way Zoya's cheeks flush as she meets my gaze.

"Your voice is funny," Logan says, breaking the spell.

Zoya giggles as I shake my head. "Logan, Zoya is from Russia. It's far away from here. She probably thinks your voice sounds funny, too."

"Sorry," he says.

"It's okay," Zoya says, holding out her hand. "Can I help you find your suitcase? Then we can get something to eat?"

Logan happily takes her hand and they walk off, Haley taking my hand as we follow along. "Is that your girlfriend?" she asks.

I wish. "No. Zoya is my friend."

"Is she special friends like Mommy has?"

A strangled sound comes out of me. "Uhhhh…no. I'm not sure what that means, exactly, but just a regular friend."

"Will you get married?"

"Haley."

"What?"

"I told you Zoya is my friend. That's all. We're not getting married."

Zoya has tuned into the conversation now. She smirks as she says, "I'm only nineteen, Haley. It is too soon to think about marriage."

"But are you in love?" Haley just won't let it go. "You look like a princess."

"Thank you, sweetie," she says, ruffling Haley's

hair, expertly avoiding the question about being in love.

The kids' attention is diverted once again when they see their suitcases coming down the conveyor belt. It's comical to see them trying to run to get to them before they pass by. I guess they don't realize they'll come back around again and again. I reach out to help them, then grab my own bag, shouldering it as we lead the kids to the driver. It's not lost on me how much easier it is to steer the kids when there's two adults to pitch in.

We pile into a Suburban—the kids in the back seat while Zoya and I sit in the middle—headed first for my apartment so we can drop the bags. Both kids are hungry, even though they ate lots of junk on the plane.

She holds my hand on the seat and I stare at it, dumbfounded. Why am I such a teenager around this woman? *Why do I hope she never lets go?*

"You okay?" she asks.

"Just really tired. It's been weird for days."

"I can only imagine."

"It means a lot that you came to meet us, Zo."

She nods at me and squeezes my hand.

All I want to do is take her hand up to my lips and kiss her there.

But I don't.

It dawns on me that although I've never had a female friend before, I don't think I've ever felt so close to *any* other friend before this either. During every conversation, I've felt her strength, her comfort, and also her confidence. *In me.* It's mind-blowing.

I've felt grounded. Calm. As though I've found a life raft. No. *She is my life raft.*

AS SOON AS we walk into the house, I take out my phone to snap photos of the main rooms, the kids' bedroom, my bedroom, the extra bedroom, and the bathroom, then send them to Winter as promised. She said they usually do a site visit, but photos would suffice to start, considering the distance.

I show the kids to their room, equipped with two twin beds and all the things Marlena has unpacked. I think the biggest excitement for them might be having their own beds. They screech and jump up and down as Zoya asks, "Two beds?"

"I always hoped they'd come to visit me some time," I answer with a shrug. "Literally no one has ever slept on those beds."

"Well, now they will." Zoya pats her hand on my shoulder. "I can help them unpack while you order some food."

"Yes, food," I say heading into the kitchen to look at my stash of menus. I end up dialing for pizza delivery. I should probably get them something healthier, but honestly, I'm too tired to think right now. I really want a nap. I wonder if that's childish of me. How the hell do parents even do this day in and day out?

Pizza ordered, I wander back into their bedroom to find Zoya reading a book that Haley brought in her backpack. All three are crammed in the space on the rug between the two beds and both kids look as tired as I feel.

"Hey, I ordered a pizza—"

"We want to go to the park!" Logan yells.

"Inside voice, bro," I say, holding my fingers to my ears.

"Sorry," he says. That's his thing, saying "sorry," but it comes out like "sawwy." It's like a four-year-old boy version of puppy-dog eyes.

"Well, I'd be happy to take you to a park to play, but I think you need a nap first."

Ever heard two kids sound like ten? Tell them they need a nap.

WITH THEIR LITTLE bellies full of pizza, and the promise of a trip to the park, they're both asleep in forty-five minutes. As soon as I shut their door, I stumble over to my couch and practically collapse down onto it.

"Holy shit." Resting my head against the back cushion, I pinch the bridge of my nose between my fingers. "I'm so fucking tired. So, so tired. This is not what I wanted, Zo. Not at all."

"Do you mean you don't want the best for your brother and sister, because I doubt that's true."

"I didn't want to be a dad."

"Well, technically, you are not a dad. You are still their big brother. A hero to them, I would guess."

"Yeah, but here I am with two kids to take care of. All because my ma…" I trail off, shaking my head. "You know I went to see her in jail. Told her I was taking the kids back with me to Vegas. She laughed in my face, Zo. Told me I'd fuck 'em up. But you know what the kids told me? That she has random guys over all the time. Strange men who disappear into her bedroom and then leave later. And the whole time they're just sitting on the couch watching cartoons and making their own peanut butter sandwiches amidst a buffet of prescription and illegal drugs."

"I am so sorry, Ty. But this is your mother deflecting from her own sins. She is trying to make you feel badly, because it's easier than looking in at herself and her own mistakes."

"You're so wise. And you called me Ty. That's cute."

"Well, you call me Zo. I thought we might be to the nickname stage of this friendship."

"I agree. We *should* be doing nicknames by now." I shake my head sadly. "But I really hate that I wasn't there to protect them."

"You are here now."

"How am I supposed to do this though? I'm gonna be traveling again soon. This job is busy. I have training, team meetings, practice, games, travel. I can't just drag them around everywhere with me."

"This does not have to be permanent, though," she says in that calm, soothing voice of hers that works wonders on my stress levels. "Do you have another relative somewhere?"

I shake my head. "There's no one else. Just me. Even their birth certificates list father unknown, and Lockhardt as their legal name. No grandparents living anymore either. My mom was an only child."

"Well, maybe you can put your mom in long-term treatment? You know, long enough to make a real change?"

"I'll think about it. We've tried rehab before, but she left after a month." I sigh. *God, I'm so tired. Just want to be fucking held right now.* "Zoya, do you mind… I… do you mind giving me a hug? Can I have a hug from my friend?" I'm not even lying. I just really need to have her close to me if even for a moment or two. There's something about her voice that calms me, makes me feel more grounded, less scattered. Her touch is the same. It soothes me in a way that nothing else ever has before. And I'm fucking desperate for it right now after everything that's gone down in the last ten days. I'm wrecked.

"Of course." Zoya sits down next to me, the scent of her flowery perfume intoxicating like a painkilling drug. I pull her to me, and we linger like that, just holding each other for the longest time. I feel like I could stay this way literally forever. It's so good having her pressed against me.

When we pull away, Zoya meets my eyes and she's biting her lip. I feel the strongest desire to kiss her. But then, *she kisses me.* It's soft, tentative. Lips on lips, her arms on my biceps. And I'm like a stone, totally frozen in place because I'm half convinced that I've actually fallen asleep and I'm just dreaming this whole situation.

Still, as Zoya pulls back, I hear myself say, "This isn't what friends do." My voice sounds odd and dazed even to my own ears.

Zoya leans back in and kisses me again, this time more urgently. Against my lips, she whispers, "Maybe it could be what friends do."

I give in. Every fantasy I've tried to hold back is at the front of my mind now when I pull her onto my lap to straddle me. Our lips and tongues explore one another while her hips move subtly against mine, my erection instant and straining to get to that magical place between her legs. God, I'm gonna fuckin' die here with her. Probably in the next few minutes. Totally cool with it, too. At least, I'll die happy with Zoya's lips kissing me and the weight of her on my lap grinding against my cock. *Christ, help me.*

From there, it evolves into a full-on make-out session. We're kissing each other's lips and necks, behind ears and the tops of shoulders. My hands are glued to her ass, hers to the sides of my face, just holding on to each other and kissing, over and over again.

At some point, in a haze, we move to lie down and end up on our sides, facing each other, her leg hooked over mine. I've never enjoyed making out so much in my life. We're totally, fully clothed and I am totally and fully turned on. I want more, so much more, but I let her set the pace. She moves one of my hands up under her shirt and I go for it, covering one perfectly round, full breast in my hand and then tweaking her nipple beneath a thin, lacy bra. I wish I could see my hand touching her right now, because I can only imagine what beauty lies under the T-shirt. This exploration is happening by feel only. When she sighs against my mouth, I swear it's nearly enough to make me come.

I need to touch her more. Feel her. I want inside her.

I move my hand down. Past her flat stomach and down farther under her jeans, but her hand puts a dead stop to mine from going any farther.

"Not yet," she says between kisses.

I try to roll away, to catch my breath.

"Tyler? Is it okay? That I want to stop there?"

"It's your call, Zo. Always your call. I just—I need a minute. To calm down."

She rolls away, stands, then perches at the end of the nearby chaise. "It's not that I don't want to do more with you. It's just that—well, I'm a virgin."

I groan and turn away, shoving my face into the pillows of my couch. "Don't tell me that." It comes out sounding more like wah-wah-wah-wah. I might actually cry.

A few deep breaths and I turn back over and force myself up into a sitting position, trying to will my raging cock under control.

"How is it possible that a woman who looks like you could be a virgin?" I can't even believe the words coming out of my mouth right now.

"Do I seem like the type who sleeps with many men?"

"Fair point. No, you do not. But still. No high school boyfriend? No raging hormones?"

She grins. "I have my vibrator. Does that count?"

Another strangled groan pops out of me. "Oh gods, woman. You are going to kill me. Today. I will be dead, and it'll be all your fault."

She giggles and calls me dramatic.

"Well, making out was wicked fun," I say, for lack of anything better. "For me at least."

"It was fun for me, as well." Her cheeks have turned dark pink and she looks…hot. Both definitions of the word, of course.

"Are you embarrassed, Zo?"

"No." Then a second later a whisper, "Well, a little."

"Why?"

"It was impulsive to do that with you. I don't want to give the wrong impression." Her golden-brown eyes stare at me, holding me captive because I just can't seem to look away from her. Ever.

"What? That we're more than friends? I get it, babe. You've put me squarely in the friend zone. I'm in no danger of thinking we could be more."

The tone of my words comes out more harshly than I intended. Blame it on the blue balls I have now. Or the fact that I haven't really slept right in the last week. Or, you know, worrying I might be getting lost in a woman who has a temporary visa to live in America. A woman who is *still a teenager.* A woman whose brother will castrate me if I touch her—especially because she's a fucking virgin. A woman who doesn't want to be in a relationship with me.

A woman I'm not sure I can live without.

And that scares me the most because of something Viktor said about his wife when I laughed in his face about falling in love. *"This English word, 'falling' in love is wrong word. In Russia, we have a phrase better suited. To selflessly choose to* love *without reservation daily. That is love for Scarlett to me."*

But I don't think I had a choice. In fact, I think falling is the right verb.

So, let's tally.

Two things I said I'd never do: fall in love and have kids.

As of today, I have two small children to raise, and I'm fairly certain I've fallen headfirst into the fountain of love with nineteen-year-old Zoya Kolochev.

Could this be true?

Yes, it can, fucker. Joke's on you... all the way to the spank bank.

For someone so sure about having nothing to do with either of those worlds, I've gone and done an epic fail.

Epic.

Fucking.

Fail.

21
thirsty

Zoya

Tyler gets up and stalks into his kitchen. He pulls out a jug of orange juice and chugs from it. I follow, nervous I may have upset him. I peer at him like he's a wounded animal that might lash out.

"You are no longer a bachelor. You can't just chug from the bottle like that. Use a cup."

"What are ya, the etiquette police?" He shakes his head but he's chuckling.

"You have to teach the kids good behaviors."

"Yeah, yeah, I know."

I suck in a breath, then shut my mouth, pursing my lips to one side. "I will give you that this apartment is really, really tidy. For a single man, and an athlete. I expected it to smell like feet."

His lips quirk at this. "Really? Am I a smelly guy?"

"No." *I love the way you smell. And now, I love the way you kiss and wish we hadn't stopped.*

"Well, then..." He shrugs. "I grew up in squalor,

Zo. I learned to be quite OCD about cleaning at a very young age."

There doesn't seem to be anything to say to that. "I—I'm sorry. For pushing you away just now. Are you surprised to hear I'm a virgin?"

He licks his lips and gives me a cocky look. "Kind of. Not really? I don't know. I try not to make assumptions about things like that, but you've never seemed like someone who was easy. It caught me off guard, but mainly because I was in a bit of a haze. You really turned me on."

I feel my cheeks heat for like the ninetieth time in the past hour. "Well, I feel the same."

He steps forward, putting his hand on my cheek. The way he looks down at me, it pools like electricity in my belly, a dark spark of magic that I just have never felt before with anyone else I've dated. I've found men attractive, sure, but never have I wanted to go this far.

"I r-really care about you, Tyler." My voice has a breathless quality to it that's embarrassing. "I always had this vision...that I would find a prince charming type. I never felt connected to other guys and I thought it was because there was this one perfect guy out there waiting for me."

"And I'm not that guy?" He has a sly grin on his handsome face. "You sure?"

"I'm not sure of anything right now. But you really are my best friend. You have become my best friend and I think...I trust you. I think I would be okay if it was you who took my virginity."

His laugh is one of surprise. He leans in to kiss me and I am surprised at how feral I get. I pull him close, parting my lips as he picks me up and sits me on the kitchen counter, his cock straining behind his jeans once more as he pushes himself in between my legs. My fingertips dig into his back. I have no self-control right now.

Abruptly though, he pulls away from me, running his hands through his hair and stabbing me with an intense gaze. "Woman, you are gonna be the damn death of me."

"I just said—"

"I know what you said. But for one, I'm probably literally the worst guy in the world for a nice girl like you to lose your virginity to. And second, I don't want you to just be *okay* with losing your virginity to me. That sounds like, *'I like brussels sprouts okay when they're cooked the right way.'* That's not sexy."

"Well, when you put it *that* way..." I push my lips out in a pout.

Tyler levels me with that dark look he sometimes gets. "Look, Smokeshow, if and when we make love, I'd want it to be so good for you. I'd want it to be very special for you, and I'd want you to feel safe. But more than that, I'd want you dripping wet and screaming for it. I'd want you thinking of nothing else other than how badly you want me inside you."

I can't stop the gasp that erupts at his beautiful, sexy words. The look on his face. The way his cock still strains beneath his jeans. My nipples go hard and my mouth dry as I pant to breathe in oxygen. Now I understand the slang term "thirsty." Yes, I am totally thirsty for Tyler Lockhardt.

"There you go," Tyler says, proud of himself. "So you see, Zoya Kolochev, that we have some work to do."

"Sexy work?"

He raises an eyebrow. "Maybe. But also, I need you to know I care about you, too. As more than a friend, just so we're clear. You mean more to me than just a quick and dirty fuck, and I won't take it for granted. I want you in my life. You're gorgeous, yes, but also caring and supportive and smart. You make me feel calmer, more steady. I'm so glad we're friends. And I wouldn't give that up for the world."

Swoon.

I have to take a deep breath to steady myself. His words go straight to my head, to my heart, to my core. *I'd want you thinking of nothing else other than how badly you want me inside you.* Alongside those words. My body is a live wire. I'm ready to begin my education right now.

It shouldn't come as a surprise to me though. I've made myself come while thinking of him before. More times than I care to admit. I've tried to box in my attraction to Tyler, to keep it limited to the times when I'm alone in my room. But here it is, and now that the box is open? It's so much harder to close down than it ever was before.

"Wow. You admit you care for a woman and that friendship is more important than sex, *and* you have custody of your brother and sister all in one week. Are you growing up, Tyler?"

"God, I hope not," he says with a laugh that turns into a yawn. "And I didn't say friendship is more important than sex. I said I wouldn't give up *our* friendship for the world. You are such a surprise to me, Zoya. A beautiful, wonderful, amazing surprise. I had no clue that anyone like you even existed in the world, let alone could be *my* friend. You came out of fuckin' nowhere and into my life... and now I need you in it.

Wow. I never expected to hear those words from Tyler's lips. About me. I do not know what to do with them right now. *Say thank you?* Acknowledge I think I might feel the same way, even though I've never had sex? Question more?

"Okay then. You need a nap?"

He nods and yawns again, so I hop down and take his hand, leading him back to the couch. He lies down and then I do, too, his arm draped over my midsection as we spoon, our bodies molding perfectly together before we drift off.

So very perfectly.

WHEN I WAKE UP, I'm on my back and Tyler is nowhere to be found. I sit up, rubbing my eyes and then checking my phone, which is on the table. *I've missed a study session with Jay.* The realization gives me a flutter of anxiety. First, because I really should have been studying today. Second, because I had possibly given Jay the impression we might go on a date. And now it feels wrong, like I would be hurting Tyler if I did. But Tyler is not my boyfriend, right? He's still just my friend and I still don't want to date someone so immersed in hockey. And then there's my sister's obsession with sleeping with him hanging over my head.

What to do, what to do...

I hear Tyler's voice and follow it back to the kitchen, where he's talking on the phone and eating lunch meat out of the package, the open bottle of orange juice back out on the counter. I hear him say, "See you later," and then he ends his call, giving me a lazy smile.

"Hey, Sleeping Beauty. Good nap?"

"Great," I say, suddenly feeling shy with him. "You?"

"Just what I needed. 'Til my pocket kept vibrating. It was Vik."

"Vik?"

"Viktor. Demoskev?"

I shake my head.

"Big fucker? Plays crash-hockey on defense with me? Played Olympic hockey with your own brother? Not ringing a bell at all?"

"I don't really follow hockey." I shrug. "Sorry."

"Well, he got in a fistfight with your brother a few years ago and it was all over the damn news."

"Oh! I do think I know who you're talking about.

His wife had a baby boy at the party, right? Pam was obsessed with him."

"Yes. He's my friend. Married a girl in the PR department. Third player in a row to break the fabled non-fraternization policy. Though, to be honest, that policy's a fuckin' joke. Literally no one adheres to it."

"Do you have relationships with the staff?" I can't stop myself from asking, and I blush again. I vow that I must learn to stop this blushing thing right this instant.

"Do you mean am I fucking anyone who is currently on staff at the Crush? No. I am not. Though I do go out with some of the sales staff sometimes."

"Oh." I want to ask if he's seeing anyone else, but I cannot bring myself to ask that question. Plus, it will look childish. Jealous. And I have no right to be jealous with him at all.

"So what did your friend Viktor want?"

"He and Scarlett are helping me find a nanny for the kids while I'm at work or on the road. They're interviewing a couple of people for me because I don't know shit about what to look for in a person like that. Viktor told me Scarlett actually said I'd probably look for the best-looking nanny so I could fuck her, can you believe that shit?"

"Well..." I raise a shoulder.

He clucks his tongue at me. "I would never."

I make a dubious noise and he glares at me.

"They're saving my life, here. Helping me get the kids into a private school where other players' kids go. There's a preschool for Logan and a first grade for

Haley. Nanny will come every morning to help get them ready for school, get them dropped off, then pick them up until I get home."

"Sounds perfect. What nice friends."

"Yeah," he says, looking away and swallowing. I think he is struggling not to show emotion. In that way, he is like my brother and father. But he manages to push it down. "I'm just happy they'll have some normalcy in their lives for a bit. A routine. Children's Services said Haley had poor attendance at her school in Boston, and Logan was never registered for preschool. I guess Haley was often home taking care of Logan. How fucked up is that? She's *six*."

My heart breaks for the two sweet kids asleep in the bedroom only feet away from us. "This is a good thing you are doing."

"I hope. I hope they don't just go right back to that shithole of a situation," he says sharply. "Fuck, it makes me so angry. I don't think Haley is even reading yet and Logan seems really fuckin' lost, poor little guy."

"Well, maybe after the park we can go out and get the kids some books and puzzles tonight. And let them pick out some things to make the room their own?"

"Good idea," he says, stepping forward to pull me into a hug. "Thanks again for bein' here. I needed it."

I needed it too, though.

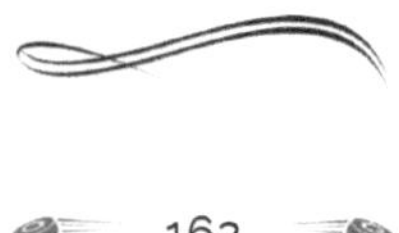

AS WE WALK toward the entrance of the store, Logan's little hand firmly in mine, Haley asks, "Are you sure you're not my brother's wife?"

"Pretty sure," I say with a smile down at her cute face looking up at me. "I think I would remember getting married."

"Come on, now," Tyler says, picking her up and setting her on his hip. "You know Zoya is just my really good friend. We talked about this."

"Well she acts like she lives with you," Haley says.

"I live on campus, in a dorm room," I answer. "I'm just a college student, too young to get married."

"Well, not technically," Tyler mutters. "I mean, you're an adult…"

I roll my eyes. "Not helpful, Ty."

"I think you'd be a pretty wife," Haley announces.

"I agree," Tyler says.

I ignore them both and head toward the book section of the store.

ONCE WE RETURN to Tyler's place, the kids ask if they can watch cartoons. Tyler says they can, for a little while, but then they need to take baths and read stories, and then go to bed. He tries to explain the time difference, but they don't get it.

While they watch shows, I spread out my statistics textbook, notes, and calculator. I have an important project due in three days and I'm way behind. Ty helps me sort out my research and put it into a spreadsheet. From there, we work through the details of the project and I can't believe how much better I understand it when he explains it to me.

Each time our eyes meet, there is a new spark there, a growing of this thing that is happening between us. It causes me some internal anxiety, to be honest. Initially, I saw him as a party boy, a womanizer, a crude hockey boy with no heart. It was easy to ignore him, to turn him down. But now? Now I want to kiss him. A lot. And I know how generous his heart is, how hard he's worked to get away from the life he had as a child. I see how much he wants to keep Logan and Haley away from that life. How much guilt he feels about how they have lived so far.

I came here looking to get as far away from hockey as possible. When I was in Russia, the hockey players always cat-called and leered at me and Irina. My sister was always loud about it, giving them the finger, shouting insults at them. I tried to dress as nondescript as possible. I'd put in earbuds and listen to music the whole time I was in the arena, just to keep from hearing it. The boys were vile and rude, and I didn't want to be around them.

My brother's behavior was just as bad, and I knew that was the culture. These were not men for me, and I wanted nothing to do with any of them. Despite Irina's feminist outlook, she tolerated these men. Wanted them. And hated them equally. For me, I was sick of the boys and their words and the culture on and off the ice. I needed to see that there were men out there who believed being a gentleman wasn't a weakness. Who believed deference to women didn't make them less of a man. Who saw that sweet words and kindness showed respect. *That's all I wanted.* And now? Now I'm here, at Tyler's kitchen table, crushing hard on the biggest hockey boy of them all. He has a reputation as a manwhore—shameless—something that's publicly splattered around the Internet. And while I believe he cares about me in his way, I don't know if it's in the way I want or deserve. I don't know if it would last, or if he's just trying to make a conquest of me.

I didn't want to feel this way, but I do. I care about him too much and maybe I just need to close the box back up, admit I had a moment of weakness, and go back to being his friend. And then, more than possibly, watch him kiss and touch other women, knowing that I could have had that if I wanted. *Knowing his body would never be a part of mine.*

We finish my statistics and I tell him I should get home. At the door, I give him a brief kiss on the cheek. His eyes search mine and the confession just tumbles out of me. "I don't know if we should let this go further."

He swallows. Nods. "Sure. Whatever you want, Smokeshow."

"It's just...I care for you very much. More than I planned. I'm in school and you are a professional athlete, but I still want to be your friend. I still will be your friend, for anything you need. But maybe we shouldn't..." I leave it hanging, a question, an implication.

"I hear you. It's fine. I meant what I said earlier. You mean the world to me. I'll take whatever I can get."

"Thank you, friend," I whisper.

He lets out a bitter sounding laugh but kisses me on the top of my head before saying goodnight and shutting the door.

It feels like a wall coming down and the hot tears sting my eyes. I want to slap myself. I'm the one who did this, who put up this barrier. Why the hell am I crying?

Pretty sure I know that answer, because Ty had shown me he was a gentleman...albeit a gentleman who kissed like a demon. He'd shown me respect, with sweet words and so much kindness. He's turned his life around for two small humans who desperately needed love in their lives.

I think I'm falling in love with Tyler Lockhardt.

If I haven't already.

22

don't you dare say her name

Tyler

It's pregame at home, my first game since coming back from Boston. I'm excited to be back, but more excited that the kids finally get to see me play. I wave to them from the ice during warmup, the nanny in between them with an armload of snacks. They wave back and the camera catches them, putting their images on the jumbotron for a moment. Nanny Patricia—who's pushing sixty and in zero danger of ever being hit on by me—points it out and their grins grow huge on their little faces as they see themselves larger-than-life on the screen.

Oddly, that moment of happiness carries me, and we have a damn good game, holding two first-period goals all the way through for a shutout.

So here's the rub. Having the kids with me means a very different post-game celebration than before. Like, I'd like to go to a club, get a little dirty dancin' on, and then have some meaningless sex with someone who looks absolutely nothing like Zoya

Kolochev. Seriously, can't get her or the feel of her lips, or the heat of her body off my goddamn mind. All we did was kiss. I copped a feel over the top of her bra. Even high schoolers would say that's nothing. But it was hot, and I felt connected to her in ways I've never felt with anyone else. And then she called me her friend again and walked out. And I've been a wreck ever since.

And because of that, I need a fast and dirty fuck. I've jacked off countless times to thoughts of her. Blasting the cannon doesn't help, unfortunately. I think I need to get laid to get her out of my head. But I can't do it tonight, because I'm having dinner in a family-friendly establishment. With my four- and six-year-old siblings.

Pam, Georg, Viktor, Scarlet, and Irina all join us at some seizure-inducing place with strobe lights and blinking games and loud noises. And chicken fingers. The kids wanted chicken fingers so now we have a table full of them.

Well, there's more than chicken fingers. There's milkshakes and other various items that our nutritionist would cringe over.

Georg and Logan are off playing a video game together, while Pam colors a picture with Haley. Scarlett has baby Alex strapped to her in some odd-looking wrap that looks complicated, though she seems totally relaxed as she talks to Irina about the #MeToo movement.

"I mean, I worked in the casinos," Scarlett is saying. "Getting my ass grabbed or having some jerk saying something obnoxious to me was pretty much a daily occurrence."

Irina has her stool pulled up close to mine, her hand on my leg. There's nothing sexual about it, but there is somewhat of an assumption of comfort level that I'm not sure I have with her. Not like I have with Zoya. I don't move away, though. Honestly, Zoya put me in the zone. I'm horny, free game, and Irina doesn't come with strings, so...

Georg brings Logan back and tells him he has to eat two chicken fingers before they can play another game. I watch, mouth hanging open, as the little guy actually shoves a chicken finger in his mouth. No whining. No negotiating. He just does it. Like magic.

"Maybe it's time for you and Pam to talk about kiddos," I say to Georg, nodding at Logan. "You got that pretty well under control right there."

"Well, I thought Pam and I made a pact when we got together that we weren't interested in having kids." He glances at Pam, who is now making silly faces at baby Alex. "But she seems to have baby lust lately."

"Having your own baby is different, though," Vik chimes in.

"It's not the kids I dislike," Georg says. "It's just that I probably wouldn't be any good at being a father."

"Well, my opinion? Any dad who loves his kids is better than no dad at all," I say, raising a toast and mouthing, "*Fuck* their deadbeat dad wherever he is."

"I do have the emotional range of a four-year-old,"

Georg says, presumably to cut the serious talk, "so I should get along with kids just fine. Right, Logan? We get along just fine."

Logan grins up at him and hands him a crayon. They color together while Logan eats his second chicken finger. Once he's finished, he jumps from the high stool and practically drags Georg off his, leading them both back to the games.

"I'm like chopped liver when that guy's around," I comment.

"Not to me," Irina says quietly, just to me, before going back to her conversation with Scarlett. She pays no attention to the kids at all, so I guess her statement is true. In fact, that's just it. She's paid *no* attention to the kids, and it's made me think of Zoya even more. If she was here, she'd be next to Haley, asking her about books and unicorns and the fun things they do with the nanny. She'd be giving Logan hugs whenever he reached his arms up to her, because he's a hugger, then giving him a toy dinosaur, just because he loves them. She'd be next to me, asking me how I'm coping, like she does in her text messages. But I'd get to look in her eyes as she asked me.

But she's not here.

And so far, I've avoided asking about Zoya, but I keep checking my phone, thinking about texting her to come join us. Irina turns back to me as I pull up Zoya's contact in my phone.

"She hates hockey," she says, by way of explanation. "You know that."

"Well, people gotta eat."

"She has a midterm to study for. I think she ordered dinner and stayed in."

"Cool."

I say the word...but I'm anything but *feeling cool* about it.

IRINA OFFERED to help me get the kids back to my place after dinner. It's way past their bedtime, so as soon as teeth are brushed and pajamas are on, they lie right down and crash the minute their heads hit the pillows. I shut the door to their room and find Irina on the couch, flipping through channels on the television.

"You want a beer?" I ask.

"That would be great, thanks."

I pad over to the fridge, opening it up and pulling out two cold ones. When I turn around though, Irina is there. *Right there.* Very close. I start to open my mouth to make a joke, but she kisses me before anything comes out of my mouth.

I start to pull away, to get some space, but she's forceful, her hand moving to rub against my cock over my jeans.

"I just want sex, Tyler," she says against my mouth. "Nothing more. No strings. I've wanted this for months."

I can't really back away any farther, otherwise I'd be inside my refrigerator. Zoya—*no!*—it's *Irina* nipping at my lips, growling, and rubbing her hand over my cock. My mind can only think of Zoya. Her sister. Oh God, no. This is wrong. It can't happen.

I push past her and take a few steps, putting the two beers on the counter. "Irina—"

"Don't you dare say my sister's name," she hisses.

"I didn't," I say, hands up in surrender. "I'm not."

She steps forward, rubbing her hand over my cock again. "I want to get you hard. Will you get hard for me?"

This is what I wanted, right? I wanted random, meaningless sex. I wanted to get Zoya out of my head. And here is a beautiful, smart, no-nonsense woman who wants exactly that. So why am I only getting semi-hard? Why am I about eighty-percent disinterested in this whole thing?

I blow out a long sigh and move Irina's hand away from my junk. "I'm sorry, Irina—I can't. You're sexy as fuck but—"

"I'm not Zoya. Got it."

She heads to the door, grabbing her bag, and saying, "I won't bother you again."

The door slams behind her and the room becomes eerily quiet.

Fuck. What trouble am I about to be in?

23
z-value

Zoya

I look at my phone for the tenth time. Where's Irina?

I'm sitting at our favorite lunch spot near campus, where she said she would meet me after class. I've called and texted and she hasn't responded, which is unlike her. There was a hockey game last night—I know she went. Maybe she went out drinking after?

I won't lie. I stayed in studying, but I probably spent a third of my time fretting over the thought of Irina going out with Tyler after the game. Now, sitting here alone with my sister missing in action, I wonder if she went home with him. I am really wondering if they slept together.

It would serve me right if they did. I could have had him, but I put him back in the friend zone. It's my actions that led to this, so I can only blame myself if my sister slept with the guy I might be falling in love with, right?

They are both consenting adults. It's not fair of me to push him away and then expect him not to want other women. Honestly, I shouldn't get worked up about this because he's not long-term relationship material anyway. We might have had fun once or twice, but he will never settle down. It wouldn't have lasted. Besides, Tyler is my friend only—I told him we shouldn't be more. He can sleep with anyone he wants.

Still, it's not like Irina to ignore my calls and texts, so I worry as I order a cup of soup, pulling out my biology book to study while I wait.

When that becomes pointless, I give up and head to class, Jay taking his seat next to mine as usual. We have been hanging out just as friends. I'm not interested in having a boyfriend or dating anyone right now. I told Jay I want his friendship, but needed to focus on my grades this semester, and he understood.

"You look worried," he says, pushing his thumb against the lines creasing between my eyes.

"I can't reach my sister. We were supposed to meet for lunch, but she didn't show, and isn't answering my texts or calls."

"Did she go out last night?"

"I think she may have gone with the hockey crowd to the game. Perhaps to watch Tyler?"

"Maybe she slept over somewhere and her phone died?"

"Maybe. It's probably that. Perhaps she slept at Tyler's..."

I trail off, flipping through my notebook, starting to doodle as the professor gives instructions for the midterm.

"And you're not okay with them sleeping together?"

"I'm okay with it."

"Have you changed your mind about him? I thought you said friend zone only. No dating hockey players, blah, blah, blah."

"I haven't changed my mind, Jay."

"Have you changed your mind about me?" he asks slyly.

I look up and he wiggles his eyebrows, giving me a wide, silly grin.

"No. Absolutely not." I stifle a giggle. "You are stupid."

"I'm not stupid," he answers, mock-hurt. "And to prove it, I'm going to read your mind. You like this Tyler, even though you don't want to. Maybe more than friends, and definitely enough that you feel resentful of your sister maybe sleeping with him."

I start a little, looking back at him. "Wow. That was…oddly accurate. Though I'll deny I ever said it if you repeat it."

He punches me lightly on the arm as the test bundle gets passed down our row. "I am a genius at reading women."

"You need to be a genius at reading biology," I tell him.

"Don't be jealous of my mad skills. Also, and I'm being serious here, you need to be honest about your feelings. If not with me, at least with yourself. This shit can get messy. If you care about him, you should tell him."

I LOOK at my phone and realize I was supposed to meet Tyler for statistics tutoring. My stomach flips, butterflies invading as I walk to the coffee shop. I half expect he won't show up—partially because Irina didn't this morning, and partially because of the way I left things with him the last time I saw him.

I swing open the glass door and scan the space, nearly breaking into tears when I see him, his back to the door, sitting across from Logan and Haley, who are happily munching cookies and drinking smoothies.

Tyler turns, almost as if he has radar, and gives me a heartbreakingly wide smile when he sees me. He stands and I'm in his strong arms, hugging him and breathing in his delicious clean scent before I even have a conscious thought about it.

"Hey, Smokeshow," he says, his chin resting on my head. "Good to see you, too."

I take a seat between the kids, and they start babbling about their experience in Vegas so far. They tell me about the hockey game, about playing video games with Georg.

"Georg is my big brother; did you know that?" I smile at them, happy to just be with all of them again. I've missed them all so much.

"I love him!" Logan yells. "He playeded video games with me."

"Played, Logan, not playeded," Tyler corrects.

"Georg," Logan says with a giggle.

Tyler looks at me and shakes his head. "He won't stop talking about Georg. It's like he's found his soulmate or something."

"That is scary."

"Right?"

I pull out my book, but the effort is futile. It's been nine days since I've seen Tyler, and every time I look at him, he steals my breath. And his little charges? I simply cannot believe the life and happiness in their eyes. They were so guarded and quiet when I first met them, yet now, after such a short time with their big brother, they are completely different. Seems like Ty has that effect on every person he meets. *Which makes staying away even harder.*

After thirty minutes of not even opening a book, Tyler says, "Sorry, Zo. Guess the kids have missed you too much. Do you want to come over and study at my place? I can call for Chinese takeout?"

"Sounds great," I say, happy to see we are okay, that he doesn't want to avoid me now after I friend-zoned him for a second time.

I'M JUST as happy to see him when he opens the door to his apartment as I was when I saw him at the coffee shop earlier.

"We should be good for at least an hour. The kids are watching a movie," he says after inviting me in. He's looking incredibly delicious in ripped jeans and a black Crush T-shirt. His cropped blond hair slightly damp from the shower, the fresh scent of soap or body wash, or whatever addicting elixir it creates when mixed with *him*, floats up my nose. I'm doomed to failure . . . I just know it. How can I concentrate on stats with him looking and smelling this good?

"Thanks for doing this, Tyler."

"I told you, *any time*, Smokeshow. You need help with stats, I am your guy."

I wish *you were my guy.*

Getting to work, I spread out my laptop and notebook. "Now, I'm having issues with the codebook dialogue," I say opening my project program on my laptop.

Tyler shifts his body closer next to mine, glancing over the tables. "Did you choose your variables of interest then run them from the procedure dialogue? Usually they have the same basic components," he shares assuredly.

"Okay, done. Next, I have a problem with the population parameter," I say getting anxious.

"What's your concern?"

"My margin of error seems low."

"The Z-value?" Tyler asks. He leans over me again, his masculine scent temporarily distracting me again, though I catch myself and refocus on the data table before he can notice.

"Yes."

"We need to add in your number of standard errors to measure the Z-value accurately. There, fixed it for you," he declares, hands tapping over my keyboard.

"So, I will achieve my desired confidence level?" I say, thinking about my own inner desires about him.

"Yeah. Your percentage confidence should be right where you want it." Tyler says it while looking deeply into my eyes.

"Okay, now let's go on to the analysis," I say, quickly clicking through the program tabs before I succumb and kiss him again.

TEN MINUTES LATER.

"What if a relationship exists between the variables in the real world, but your test found no significant relationship?" He quizzes me in preparation for my project presentation. The words "relationship" and "real world" hanging in the air, heavy with implication. I wonder if he hears those words as loudly as I do?

"I would be making a false negative error?" I ask, unable to stop staring at his chiseled jawline, or keep my heart from melting.

"Right, you'd think it doesn't occur, when in fact, it does."

The implications are not lost on either of us, as we keep staring intently into each other's eyes.

Almost on the hour, the kids enter and announce

they are hungry, so Tyler calls for takeout. We sit at the table together for the meal, the kids again talking up a storm. When he tells them it's time to start getting ready for bed, he looks at me, but I don't know how to read his expression.

"Are you okay? You have a weird look on your face."

"I'm fine," he says, shaking his head like he's trying to shake away a thought.

"Well, for what it is worth, I appreciate your technical assistance. Even just a little time with you, and I feel completely prepared for my stats project presentation. You are a terrific tutor. And, as it turns out, a pretty good dad-brother, too."

"I just want to be a regular brother," he says glumly.

"Well, they need more right now. And they are happy, so I think you've been nailing it."

He grins, almost shyly. "Well, I have learned one thing. I am definitely not ready to be a real dad yet. Not by a long shot. Someday, maybe—which is a huge change of tune for me—but not right now. It's a lot of work. A lot of lifestyle adjustment."

"Well, a break from your recent lifestyle might have been a good thing," I say with a shrug.

"Maybe. I need to figure something out, though. Something long-term, and not back with our mom. I don't think I can really do this right now. Not alone and so early in my career, you know? I travel too much. They're not pets. I can't just board them every time I leave town. They deserve better—better than the life they had with my mom. Also better than what I can give them right now."

"They seem really happy, Ty. They are enjoying being here with you."

"They're great," he says sincerely. "Honestly, super awesome. I'm sure this is, like, a big vacation for them. But what's next? Where do they go? They need something stable and permanent. Normal. In a normal house with normal parents."

"Well, I think they only need someone who loves them and puts them first. Really it's all any of us need if you think about it."

He reaches out and messes my hair. "You are wise beyond your years, Zo. Oh, and speakin' of which, I took your advice. I called the courts and offered to pay for my mom to go into a one-year rehabilitation program as soon as she finishes her sentence. So, who knows? Maybe I do this for the next two, three years and when she gets well, I can find them all a place here in Vegas so I can keep an eye on 'em. Wouldn't that be something?"

I can tell he's trying to talk himself into this idea, that he maybe doesn't believe it can actually happen. After all, his mother has been in and out of rehab already. She always falls back into bad, old habits. The kids always suffer for it. I can see how he would be nervous bringing the possibility of that drama so close.

"I think you did the right thing, but the right thing can also change, over time, so maybe take small steps. The path will reveal itself."

"You Zen master." He smiles at me and my heart does that thing I'm getting very used to it doing. It bounces around inside my chest like an excited puppy.

"I know this is all a big change. Do you miss your life before? Sleeping with random women, partying all the time?"

Tyler licks his lips as he looks at my face. It makes me blush. "No," he finally says. "I think that part of my life might be over now. If nothing else, this is a wake-up call. I need to be a better role model for Haley and Logan. They need someone substantial in their lives. If it's gotta be me, then it's gotta be me."

"Well, you are a good man, Tyler Lockhardt. You really are."

"You have helped. Seriously. Your friendship has helped. You mean a lot to me."

I open my mouth, but nothing comes out. I'm overwhelmed, suddenly, and I really, really want to kiss him. I lean in. He leans in. And just as our mouths meet, the door to the kids' bedroom opens with a squeak. The sound of a crying boy fills the space.

Scooping Logan into his arms, Ty asks him what's wrong. He takes Logan to the couch, comforting him while he tells Ty about a scary dream with a "mean man." Poor baby. This source behind Logan's dream is going to wreck Tyler. I feel like now is not the time for me to intrude. He needs some privacy with his family, and I really shouldn't make a mistake I can't take back by staying here with him. So... I kiss first Logan and then Ty on the head before telling him I need to get back to the dorm.

I let myself out quietly and order an Uber to take me back. All the way home, I fret over what almost just happened. We almost kissed. We started to. Would it have gone further? Would I have wanted it to?

I'M SO DISTRACTED by my own thoughts that I barely notice my room is unlocked when I return. Inside, I find my sister sitting on my bed, her face red, her lips set in a deep scowl.

"Were you with him just now?" she asks accusingly.

"Hello to you, too. Where were you earlier? We were supposed to meet for lunch and you never showed up, never called, never texted."

"Did you sleep with him, Zoya?"

"Did *you* sleep with him, Irina?"

"Answer me first."

"No." I throw my hands up in the air. "No, I did not sleep with him. He's been tutoring me in statistics. We are just friends."

"Well, tell him that, because he flat-out rejected me last night. Because of *you*."

"Rina—"

"Don't Rina me. He's in love with you, Zoya. How can you be just friends if you're in love with each other?" I can't deny something like that to my sister.

She has always been able to read me. I don't want to think about what Irina did to have Ty reject her either, because I know how forward she is. So, I need to pass it off.

"Whatever," I say, rolling my eyes. "He's not in love with me. I know he's not. And besides, he doesn't even know *how* to love a woman. At least, not the way I want someone to love me anyway. He's a good man and he is my friend, but it's not like that between us."

"I know he's a good man," Irina says, frustrated. "I like him, too, but it's obvious he wants you. I only wanted to sleep with him. It shouldn't have hurt like that when he rejected me, but it did, and it's because I know he wanted you instead."

That's the second time she's said that, so I know Irina tried very hard to get Ty to have sex. *I cannot ask how far. I think my heart would be broken if he did with Irina what he did with me.*

"I am sorry, sister. I can't help that he didn't want to sleep with you." I barely scrape the words past my lips.

"You don't have to be sorry," she snaps. "I'll get over it."

This makes me laugh. "Well, I'm sure you will. But listen, you are *luchshaya sestrav mire*. More important than any guy. I love you."

"You're the best sister ever, too," she says, sticking her tongue out. "Even though you need to stop letting random assholes ogle you like you're a toy for their entertainment."

"Well, you need to shave your armpits."

We devolve into a fit of silly insults and giggles until we're both crying and hugging.

"I don't want you to sleep with Tyler," Irina says as we lie on my bed, side by side. "Is that bad of me?"

"Well, I promise not to," I say.

"Really?" she asks hopefully. And I hate the reason she is hopeful. *Does she really have that right to ask that of me?* Can I deny my sister anything? *No.*

"Really." I hold out my pinkie. She crooks hers and we pinkie swear.

When she leaves, I sit for a long time, thinking about the promise I just made to my sister.

And I wonder if I will be able to keep it.

24
whose face?

Tyler

April

Okay. The kids are off to school with the nanny and I still have three hours before I need to be at a team meeting at the arena. Today is going just swimmingly.

There is a lot of shit around my house now. Toys, books, snacks. Kids make a lot of messes. It's honestly fucking with my OCD tendencies, so I pace around, picking things up, organizing. I have Marlena coming now twice a week, but damn, I cannot take this clutter in between.

As I'm dumping an armload of toys into a bin in the kids' room, the doorbell rings. It's got to be Nanny Patricia and the kids—maybe they forgot something for school. I swing the door wide and, nope, it's not Patricia and the kids. It's Zoya.

Sweet, beautiful Zoya. Her hair is in two long braids and she wears a black dress with thin straps and flip-flops. She looks exactly like the sweet young coed she is, and I nearly pop wood just looking at her. It's so wrong.

"Hey," I say. She bites her lip, looking unsure. "Come in?"

"I love my sister. I would never do anything to hurt her," she blurts, still standing in the hallway.

"Oh-kay?"

"I just came to tell you that."

"Well, do you want to step inside?" I ask. "Because I'm gonna need a little more, here. You came all the way here from campus to tell me you love your sister? What's that got to do with me?"

"I cannot believe you rejected her," she says. "Irina is smart and strong and beautiful. She is confident. She knows who she is. And maybe more importantly, she knows what she is doing with a man. She knows how to pleasure a man."

"Ahh." Nodding slowly, realization dawns on me. Irina must have shared being upset about the other night. "Okay. Well, first, you're right about all those things. She's great, your sister. But...she isn't what I want. And I told you the other night, I'm not really into cheap sex anymore."

"Well, I won't sleep with you either," Zoya says, her chin jutting out like she dares me to argue with her. It's pretty cute, in all honesty. Makes me want to kiss her. A lot.

I can't help the smirk that twists at my lips. "Well, thank you for letting me know, but I don't think I ever asked you for sex."

Her eyes narrow, lips purse, hands form balls at her sides. "Good. I'm glad we cleared that up."

I'm still smirking, taking in her bravado, her little braids, her banging body. I can't help the effect she has on me. And she can't help noticing.

Zoya points at my crotch, my cock straining beneath my athletic shorts. "What's that? Why are you hard?"

"Because you turn me on?"

She steps toward me, still pointing. "If I turn you on, then why are you saying you don't want to have sex with me?"

I let out a surprised laugh. "You are the most confusing woman I've ever met, bar none. You kiss me, then you leave. You tell me you don't want me, won't sleep with me, then stand around pointing at my cock. You want me. You don't want me. Woman, you're givin' me whiplash here."

"I never said I didn't want you," she answers softly. "I only said I wouldn't sleep with you. Because I love my sister."

"Yes, okay then." I hold my hands up. "And I want to be clear. I never said I didn't want to sleep with you. I only said I never asked you to."

"Well, I don't want you, so make it stop." She pouts.

"I can't just make it stop. You have to go away. It's you making it do that, Zo. That's the effect you're having on me right now."

She steps closer still, her nostrils flaring, teeth gritted. "So you *do* want me?"

"Duh, yes."

"I lied, then. I want you too, but I'm not supposed to. I'm not supposed to want you, Ty." Her words come out desperate...like a cry for help.

IT'S ON.

I pull her to me, my lips on hers before she can say another dumb fucking thing. I kick the door shut and we stumble, kissing, pulling off our clothing, as we make our way to my bedroom. She's in only her bra and panties as I gently push her to the bed, taking in the length of her supple frame. Her legs are so, so long...smooth golden tanned skin. Her belly is flat, a small rebellion of a bellybutton piercing there. I kiss all of her body. Her shoulders and arms, her fingertips. I kiss her clavicle, the sensitive skin behind her ear. Her inner thighs. The tops of her feet. I haven't taken this much time exploring a woman's body in—well, in longer than I should admit—but with Zoya, I want to. I want to learn her body, what makes her moan, what makes her arch her back with desire, what makes her nipples harden to sharp peaks that I can barely stop myself from biting.

I've left those parts to last. When trailing kisses up from her stomach, I search her face for a sign to stop. I know this is her first time. I want her fully here, fully engaged with me. I don't see any doubt in her sparkling brown eyes.

Thank fuckin' God.

I kiss the soft skin where her tits peek above the line of her black strapless bra. She didn't come here for sex, this much I know. She meant to tell me it wouldn't happen. Couldn't happen. But now she arches into the attention, moaning softly as I unclip the front clasp of her bra, popping it open, exposing two perfectly round, fucking stunning breasts.

Groaning at the sight of her soft, flushed beauty, her pebbled nipples standing at attention, I dive in, licking and sucking and nipping. Devouring her tits, really, if we must put a term to describe what I'm doing. I can't help myself and as Zoya writhes underneath me, her hand moving to stroke at my cock, jutting hard inside my boxer briefs, I don't think she can either.

This *is* happening.

She scissors her legs, her knees bending and straightening until they fall open spread wide below me. Her eyes are bright, and her cheeks are flushed as she begs me for something I'd have to be dead to be able to deny her. "Please, please, Ty, kiss me, touch me. Please. Make me come."

It's only the briefest moment until my brain catches up. I'm in a haze of lust. Want. Desire. Maybe even more than that. She's like the best drug. When I realize what she means, the permission she's giving, I help her shimmy from her blue, lacy panties, nearly passing out at the sight of her pussy, just the barest strip of hair, her swollen clit and lips exposed and ready to take me. Oh fuuuuck, the imagery of knowing she's untouched does something to me I know is permanent. Being intimate with Zoya is going to change me.

I kiss her thighs again, slowly making my way up to kiss lightly at her pretty pussy, sliding my tongue in to taste her. She's so, so soft, so wet already. And she tastes like the sweetest, sexiest sin. At the first touch of my tongue she stiffens, so I hold still until she relaxes. Then I press my mouth up against her lovely cunt again and go in deeper. I use my hands to hold her legs wide as I suck at her clit, agitating with my teeth when it swells right along with her moans of pleasure.

She begs me some more in her sexy Russian accent, "Please, Ty. Please...make me come." Sooo fucking hot.

"Oh, I will, baby. I plan on it." I start by stroking her folds, just the tip of my finger playing at her sex as her hips sway. God, she's off-the-charts responsive. There's so much I want to do to her. I want to pleasure her until she doesn't know her name anymore.

I push my finger inside. "So tight. Is this okay?"

"Mmmmm," is the affirmative sound she makes as I move one finger in and out, slowly at first, but picking up the pace as she whispers one important word in my ear. "More."

Enraptured at the sight of her, I finger her, going faster and faster, then inserting a second finger. She's so wet, so wild, as she tweaks her nipples with her fingertips.

"Have you ever come before?"

She nods, a gasp or sigh or some combination of

the two escaping the back of her throat as her hips fly off the bed, my fingers still pushing her toward the edge. "Only by myself."

"I feel honored." Then I growl the question, "Who did you think of? Whose face did you see when you came, Zo?"

She groans, nonsensical, her eyes closed, her features tight as her pussy starts to clench around my fingers. "Oh, so close. I'm so close. Please."

"Whose face?" I demand again harshly. I need to know who to kill later.

She thrashes, her head shaking back and forth on the bed, her hair coming loose from her braids. Suddenly, her eyes open wide and she meets my gaze. "Yours..." she breathes just as a cry of ecstasy throws her over the cliff we've just climbed together. As she falls over the edge, she stops breathing, nearly levitating, her whole body rigid and trembling, her pussy clenching tight around my fingers, her whole body in a viselike grip of pleasure.

This is enough for me. I know I could stop now and oddly, be satisfied. It's never been like that for me before, but with her sex feels like...something different. Something far better than I've ever experienced.

Zoya's trembling calms as her orgasm subsides, aftershocks still rocking inside her as I slowly remove my fingers, slick with her arousal. She smiles and looks at me, dreamy, lethargic, thoroughly satisfied.

"It's never been like that," she moans. "Never as good."

"I can do that for you all the time, baby. I could watch you come for hours."

She blinks her eyes at me, a look of pure undiluted sexy takes over her expression. I know what she's going to ask. "Can you...can we— "

"Are you sure?"

"I'm sure. I want you inside me." She bites at her bottom lip and reaches for my cock.

Holy fuck. "Just so you know, I'm clean. We get tested all the time, so you don't have to worry about that, okay? I'm also going to wrap up."

"I'm on birth control," she says softly.

"That's good, but still I wanna be extra safe with you because you deserve it." Leaning in, I kiss her mouth and tug off my shorts at the same time, my dick so hard it jerks and bobs in her direction while I dig for a condom from the bedside drawer. As I'm rolling it down my length, she stares fascinated at the raging monster that is my cock right now. Does great things for my ego having her eyes on me, looking like she wants what I'm selling.

"It's big," she says, never taking her eyes away from my cock.

I love you.

"It's gonna hurt. At first. Sharp pain just as I push all the way in. You just breathe through it and I'll give you a minute to adjust. You tell me when to move." And fucking hell, that better be quick as it's been months since I've been inside a woman.

I can't even remember the last faceless girl I fucked, and honestly? I'm glad. But my balls are ready to release a long-ass time of pent-up need. My cock has wanted inside this woman from the first moment I saw her. And he has never had to wait like this before.

God, I want this woman more than breathing.

She nods as I position myself between her legs, the first touch of my cock to her pussy nearly burns us both. I kiss her again, swollen lips, her jaw, down to the hollow of her throat. She pushes her tongue into my mouth, moaning, her hands moving along my back, down to my ass. She pushes me forward and I slowly but firmly bury my cock inside her. It's tight as I fill her, her fingernails digging into my backside with a soft gasp.

"Hurt me," I say. "Scratch me. Claw me. Whatever you need."

"I'm ready," she says, an errant tear rolling down her cheek.

I kiss it away and vow to remember the taste of her virgin tears. Zoya's virgin tears when she gave herself to me for the very first time.

"Are you okay? Are you hurting, baby?"

"Only a little."

I nod, lavishing her mouth with kisses, distracting her as I start to move, slow pumps in and out of her tight, wet cunt, ready to explode already. *Fuck.* I'm never going to last any time at all because she feels so good. Perfect. *Made for me.*

I go slowly, partly because I don't want to hurt her, but also because I don't want to come yet. I want to make her come again, though. I want her to love sex, to want more of it...with me. I want her to want me. I want more from her than just this today.

When she starts to roll her hips to meet my thrusts, her eyes closing, that dreamy expression returning to her beautiful face, I know we're good. I pick up the pace, in and out, filling and retreating. I flip to my back, bringing her along so she's straddling me. Her breasts move free, fully naked and so, so beautiful. I sit up slightly, taking a nipple into my mouth, sucking hard as she cries out, her movements on top of me increasing as she learns what feels good, how this works. I let her move at her own place, exploring her own desire. Her movements start to deepen, her hips rolling, her clit brushing against the base of my cock as she starts rocking into another climax.

When she comes again, it seems to surprise her. Her eyes go wide as her hungry cunt clenches hard around me, her back arching, her tits shaking as she trembles in intense pleasure.

On a whim, I pull the bands from her braids and she shakes her hair free, so it falls in waves down her back.

"You're a goddess. Perfection."

She's crying out, closing her eyes, shaking her head, biting her lip. It's like she's having a fit of pleasure and it's a magnificent sight. *I'm gonna come.* My balls go tight and I lose control, coming right along with her, my cock pulsing and jerking inside her as I say her name, over and over and over again.

"Zoya. Zoya. Fuck. Zoya."

Collapsing, Zoya rests her head on my chest, breathing heavily. "Your heart is beating very fast," she says after a time. It could be minutes or years. I can't move nor do I want to.

"You did that to me." My lips kiss the top of her head.

She falls to the side, slipping free of me and lies on her back, her body glistening with sweat, the room full of the scent of some really spectacular fucking. Her hair is everywhere, splayed on the pillows, in her face, in my face. She's a feast of carnal loveliness.

After a minute of taking in the sight of her, I make a point to seal it in my memories. I have to remember this. I never want to forget.

I SIT UP, pushing off the bed to get rid of the condom in the bathroom. After, I wet a towel and return to press the cool relief against her swollen pussy.

"So sweet, taking good care of me." She puts a hand to my face and freezes me in place with just that light, simple touch. Zoya has superpowers with me that no other woman has. True fact.

"You feeling okay? Any pain?"

"I am fine," she answers with a shy smile. "That was...wow."

"Wow good?"

"Do you really have to ask? I didn't expect I could...you know...come...the very first time."

"Well, proved you wrong. Yay, Tyler."

She slaps my arm lazily. "Come lie with me?"

I look at my phone. I still have an hour before I need to get to the arena, so I slip onto the bed with her, pulling her naked, amazing body toward me, spooning her as we both catch our breath from what I think may have been a life-changing experience for both of us. And it has to happen again. We are not one-and-done. This woman. In my bed. My cock in her body. Her heart in my hands...*forever.* Because I know now, there will never be another woman for me. Just this beauty. *Mine.*

25

worth it

Zoya

I wake up to the sound of banging. Where am I?

Sitting up, I realize I'm naked and alone in Ty's bed. There's a general achiness between my legs and I realize what happened wasn't just a really amazing dream or a fantasy. I've lost my virginity. To Tyler Lockhardt.

There is no time to process, to analyze, because someone is knocking at the door and I can hear water running in the bathroom. Ty must have somewhere to be.

I don't really know where my clothes are, though I do find my panties close by. As I pull them on, the banging sounds more insistent, so I just grab a Crush hoodie of Ty's that I find hanging in his closet. Pulling it on, it's like a dress. I drown in it, but whatever. I like that it smells of him.

I pad out to the living room and swing the door open wide.

My brother standing on the other side looking like an angry god bent on vengeance. Georg is here.

My body goes cold, the color surely draining from my face as my brother takes in the sight of me, hair wild, dressed only in Ty's hoodie. Oh my God.

"What the fuck, Zoya? What's going on here?"

"Nothing." But we both know that's a lie. Jutting my chin forward, I tell my brother, "None of your damn business. And what are you doing here?"

Just then, Ty comes out, dressed in a nice shirt and dress pants. "I can explain—"

Crack! Georg punches Tyler in the nose. His fist making contact and the sickening sound of bone meeting flesh. Tyler throws his hand over his nose, now bleeding profusely onto his hand and down his arm.

"Get dressed," my brother growls, teeth bared like an animal. "Get dressed and come with me."

"No! You hurt him, Georg. No, we should talk about this like adults. Oh my God, we are all adults."

"I won't sit here and talk about how he defiled my little sister," Georg snarls.

"I didn't defile her," Ty says, recovering a bit, his voice nasally and wet. "Georg, I care about her."

"I told you to stay away from him." Georg points at me sharply.

"You did not. You knew we were friends. That he's been helping me with stats. You knew."

"Well then, I told *him* to stay away from *you*," he bites out, switching his pointing to focus onto Tyler.

"And you said *friends*. Friends, Zoya! Not fuck buddies."

"We are not…" I can't even say the word. "We are not that. It's more with us. I care about him and he cares about me."

"He cares about pussy! You're just a fresh piece of ass to him!"

Tyler bristles at the accusation. "Hey man, that's not true at all—"

"Shut the fuck up!" Georg yells. "Zoya, I will not tell you again. You get dressed and come with me."

There is quiet menace in his voice as his body shakes with rage. I have only seen my brother this angry a few times in my life and it is terrifying enough that I put up no more fight. It's not that I think he would ever hurt me—he wouldn't—but in all likelihood he would, in fact, do more than just make Tyler's nose bleed, and I can't have my Ty hurt any more than he already is.

So, I make a decision. I say nothing to my brother. I just walk through the apartment, finding my clothing, dressing hastily in Ty's bedroom. When I emerge, my head hangs low as I pass Tyler, who gives my hand a clandestine squeeze as I pass him by, leaving him behind, heading out his front door, my brother stomping furiously along behind.

By the time I shove myself into the front seat of Georg's BMW, I am sobbing. When Georg pulls out his phone and tells Siri to "Call Papa," I cry even harder. My father isn't going to let me stay here if he knows I've slept with a hockey player. I might as well pack my bags right now. In Russian, Georg rattles off what he has seen, me barely dressed, clothing strewn about Tyler's apartment. He knows we slept together, even after he told us to stay away from each other. I can hear my father yelling on the other end, Georg telling him over and over he has been paying attention, that he told us to stay away from the hockey players.

When he hangs up, he says, "I'll drop you at the dorm. Papa's booking a flight now. He's coming to get you and Irina to take you back."

"It's the middle of the semester," I rage at him. "I have classes to finish. I like it here."

"Well, you knew the conditions. You knew Papa wanted you to stay away from the hockey players. And...what a hypocrite. You can't come watch me play because you want nothing to do with hockey, and then you're up here screwing a player? Real nice, *mladshaya sestra*."

"I didn't mean for this to happen, Georg. He needed a friend. He needed someone to talk to, and he really did help me with my statistics. We became friends. It had nothing to do with hockey. We don't talk ever about hockey."

"Yeah, *duh*," Georg sneers angrily. "Somehow I'd guess that hockey is the last thing on your minds when you're both naked."

"This was the first time." My voice shakes a little to admit it. "*My* first time."

My brother's mouth hangs open. "I'm sorry? Come again? Did you just tell me you gave up your V-Card to Tyler Lockhardt? Are you fucking kidding me?"

"It was my choice to make. My body. I can make my own choices about this."

"Well"—he lets out a hysterical laugh—"you obviously can't, Zoya. Seriously. I might have expected this out of Irina, but you?"

"Me what? I am the quiet one? The good girl. The one who studies all the time and never parties. Well, that may be true, but I also have the right to fall in love."

"In *love*?" Georg snorts. "That's the most ridiculous thing I have ever heard you say. I can guarantee you that nothing I've seen shows that Lockhardt could ever love anyone."

"Really? Have you not seen him take in his little brother and sister recently? You did not see him take two small children into his home in order to give them a better life? Is that not love?"

"That's different. Zoya, he treats women like garbage."

"So did you. You treated women like garbage before Pam. Who says he can't change, as you did?"

"Even if I thought he could change, which I do not, it's not up to me. The judge here is Papa, and he will never care about anything other than you disobeyed him. You'll be on a flight home to Saint Petersburg in twenty-four hours, I guarantee it."

"You didn't have to call him, brother. You could've had my back."

"I'd have your back if you got caught smoking weed in the dorm. Or spray-painting graffiti on the side of a building. I am not having your back for sleeping with one of the nastiest guys I've ever met."

"Ty is not nasty. That's the pot calling the kettle black!"

Georg pulls in front of my dorm, turning off the engine. He runs a hand through his long hair and sighs, then bangs both hands on the steering wheel. "Fuck, Zoya. I can't believe you did this. And what about Irina? I thought it was Irina who liked him that way?"

I don't admit the guilt that washes over me. I made a promise to Irina that she meant more to me than Tyler. That her feelings were important to me. And yet I waltzed right over to him and into his bed. I am not sure how to deal with the guilt I feel over that, actually. Especially when I consider the joy I felt when he showed me how much he wanted me. Not my sexy sister. *Me. And now Georg has taken that away. Pridurok!*

Still, there is nothing left to say to my brother, my betrayer, except, "Fuck you, Georg."

Then I open the door and step out, slamming it before he can say another thing to me. It will be a very long time before I can even speak to my brother again.

As I walk back to my room, the tears continue. Several of my neighbors stop and ask if I'm okay. One says, "Guys are not worth the emotion," and I nod in agreement, even though I'm not sure I agree.

When I collapse onto my bed, I'm certain I don't

agree. Tyler *is* worth it. He made me feel special and beautiful. And he made me feel good and desirable and beautiful.

The thought of not seeing him again makes me sick and sad and I can't do anything but curl into a ball on my bed and cry some more.

26
mean left hook

Tyler

"Cracked you good," the team doctor says. "What'd you do to piss off ole Georgie?"

I shrug, not willing to admit I slept with "ole Georgie's" virgin baby sister. I look at my watch, grimacing because I've now missed the team meeting. "Is it broken?"

"Yes, sir," he says. "Ice it twenty minutes on, twenty minutes off. Take some Ibuprofen. Doesn't look like it needs to be realigned."

"Well, that's some good news." I sound more sarcastic than I mean to be.

"It is," he says. "Means you won't have Coach Brown on your ass for missing more ice time. Any pain elsewhere? See stars when it happened?"

"No. I mean, it hurt like a bitch but Kolochev isn't that strong. I guess it snapped my head back a bit. Some neck and shoulder pain, but nothing I can't manage."

"Welp. Go see PT just to be safe. Have them give you an ice pack."

I stand and he claps me on the back as he shoves me out the door. Next stop physical therapy, where Pam is the only one not busy working on someone at the moment.

"Why so glum, chum?" she asks as I sulk over to her table.

"Why the broken nose, you mean? Oh, that would be thanks to your husband."

She snorts. "What on earth?"

"I..." I can't help the grimace. "I need you to loosen up my shoulders and neck."

"Hmm. Well, okay. No need to be cryptic *and* sullen."

"You'd be sullen, too, if Georg just hit you in the nose."

"I'd be in divorce court if Georg hit me in the nose," she says. Then she purses her lips to one side. "Well, except for that one time, when we were trying a Christian Grey kind of thing with ropes and he accidentally knocked me in the nose with his elbow."

"La la la la la," I sing. "TMI, Pam. No need for the overshare. He does have a mean left hook, though."

"Well, it takes a lot to get him angry enough to throw a punch. So you either slept with his sister or you slept with his other sister. Those are my guesses. So, which one was it, Locksey?"

"Zoya."

Pam cuffs me on the back of the head.

"Ow!" I yelp, rubbing my head. "This is abuse."

"You idiot. The baby? Zoya is the baby of that family, dumbass. Barely an adult. Yep, that'll do it."

"See, that's the thing. She's *not* a baby, and she *is* an adult. Like...she's almost twenty. And I care about her. A lot."

"Really? When you say you care about her, can you actually think of reasons why? Like, non-body-part reasons?"

"She's sweet. Smart. She's easy to talk to. I trust her. She's like a humor ninja. She's amazing with kids. She knows when to ask for help and how to say thank you. She makes me feel...calmer, somehow. She doesn't judge me or my past. She doesn't care that I play hockey. How's that for reasons?"

Pam looks surprised but covers it quickly, telling me to lie down on my stomach. She works at the knots in my back and neck quietly for a few minutes. It's me that can't keep my mouth shut.

"I know she needs time, you know? She's young. Not a baby, but young, and she has goals. She takes school seriously. I never did and I don't want her thinking she should throw it all away for anything or anyone. I don't want her to feel trapped, you know? I want her to be happy, and her friendship means a lot to me. I feel so comfortable with her. I don't wanna lose that."

Pam pats me on the back and has me sit up so she can do some arm stretches. "Sounds like you might really have feelings for her," she finally says.

"I do. I really do. And, you know, she was a virgin when we..."

Pam's eyebrows shoot up into her hairline. "Really?"

I give her one nod. "She came to tell me we couldn't. She didn't want to hurt Irina. But...I don't know, I think we both knew something was there for a while and...it just happened."

"And it was more for you? Than just a quick lay? Sorry, I know that's personal."

"It's a fair question. And yes." I pause. How do I express that for the first time ever, I wanted to take my time? Wanted to make it good for her. More than good. How do I say that it felt like home, being with her...the first home I've felt in a long time...ever? "It was everything I've never had before, Pam. Something I never want to lose." *But due to your husband, I have no clue what will happen next. And the radio silence from Zoya hasn't helped.* "I need to know she's okay."

We're quiet for a moment, then I bust out laughing. "Wow, I sound whipped. Holy shit."

"You sound like you're in love."

I open my mouth to argue but find I can't do it, so I snap it back shut.

"Given my loyalty lies with my husband, I think I'll pause it there about Zoya. I don't know what's going to happen now, Tyler, but it probably won't be good."

"Yeah, fuck I know that." But I have no idea what I can do to change this.

Pam changes the subject, God love her. "How are the kids?"

I groan a little. "They're good kids. Doin' real well,

yeah? You know they haven't asked about her, not once? It's insane."

"It's sad, that's what it is," Pam mutters. "Will they have to go back?"

"If she agrees to go to treatment and comes out clean, she can get them back. I'm planning to bring her out here for a one-year program. Maybe set them all up with a place here after that, so I can keep a closer eye."

"That's a reasonable and admirable plan, Tyler, but what if rehab fails? What if things just go back to the way they were?"

"I don't know. I'll cross each bridge as I come to it, I guess. I need a long-term solution but it's not clear to me yet what it is. What is clear however, while I do love my siblings, I was in no way qualified to do this, and in no way ready to be their parental guardian. And I travel too much to be of any use. They spend more time with the nanny than they do with me. It's nuts. You know what I mean?"

"I think you're doing the best you can, and that your best is a far cry better than what they had before. You're doing a good thing, here."

I hop off the table and salute her. "Thanks for listening."

She nods and I head out, down the hall, grabbing the elevator up to the coaches' suite. When I walk in, black eyes blooming, tape on my nose, Coach rolls his eyes at me.

"What the fuck, Lockhardt?"

"Sorry, Coach, I—"

"That was rhetorical. Look, shit happens, but we are two home games away from the playoffs. We're in contention here and every damn body is watching every move. I need you there and one hundred percent in the game, so where is your head?"

"I'm committed, Coach. We've all worked too damn hard to let this season slip away. I promise, I've got my shit together. I'm here for it."

He nods. "Good. Now get out of here."

27
hypocrites all

Zoya

Nauseous. That's how I feel as I watch Kirill Kolochev walk toward me in baggage claim at the airport. I figured it was best to face my executioner and meet him straight away.

My father is a handsome man, his dark, curly hair clipped short, graying at the temples. He's tall and broad-shouldered, sharply dressed in a white button-down shirt, gray slacks, and a blue suit jacket.

As handsome as he is, nothing can cover the downturn of his mouth, deepening with each step he takes toward me. My stomach is a pit of acid.

He steps toward me, pulling me into a fierce hug that belies how livid I know he must be. He pulls away, scanning my face. *"Ty khorosho vyglyadush', doch'."* *You look well, daughter.*

"English, Papa," I remind him.

He wraps his arm around my shoulders, and we walk along, his roller bag bumping along behind us. I call for a town car and we wait only a few minutes.

Once we're inside, though, he turns to me and says, "What were you thinking?"

"I was thinking I'm an adult and allowed to make my own choices."

"You were specifically told to stay away from wild hockey boys and yet you picked the wildest of the wild to sleep with. Zoya, this is not proper behavior. It is not good for you."

"Papa, I'm nearly twenty. I work hard in school. I don't get in trouble. I think I can choose what is good for me."

"Tyler Lockhardt?" he asks, giving me a face. "Really? Zoya, I did not send you here to sleep with Georg's hockey teammates. I sent you to get an education. I gave you one strict condition and you broke it."

"I have been focused on my education, Papa. You told me to get a tutor and I did—it just happened to be Tyler. We became friends, and then later...something more."

"More. Meaning you slept with him. It disgusts me."

Gritting my teeth, I look away, taking a breath to avoid lashing out. *It disgusts him?*

"I cannot have you sleeping around," he continues. "I will have you to come home immediately."

"I'm not sleeping around. I fell in love. I made love to someone I care about." My cheeks heat as I make this admission out loud.

My father snorts. "This is not love, daughter. This

is lust, and while I am not so old to forget how our hormones rage when we are young, I also thought you had more sense. I thought you would be more practical."

"More practical than whom? Than Georg, who slept his way through three countries before settling down? Than Irina, who is smart and talented, and choosing to control her own body and choices?"

"More practical than to give yourself away to the first man who looks at you."

A strange, choking, gasp of a laugh rattles its way up through my chest. "The first man who looks at me? Are you blind, Papa? I get looks every day, all day. I have men ask me out all the time, and I have chosen, mostly, to say no. Why? Because I'm serious about my studies, about my goals. Because I don't throw myself around for male attention and I never have. Of all people, you should trust me most when I say that what I feel *is* real."

"You are only nineteen," he argues.

"You were only a teen when you met Mama. Don't be such a hypocrite."

"*Eto bessmyslenno*," he growls. "Why throw everything away for this one man, who will surely leave you crying?"

"Who said anything about throwing anything away?" I ask, angry tears rolling down my cheeks. "What if he adds to my life? What if he makes my life better? Happier?" And what if you taking me home to Russia is what causes me to throw everything away?"

"You are too young to understand, *milaya*

devushka." My father runs a hand through his hair and sighs. "He will love you and then leave you. Your head will spin and your heart will break. I know these players. I know the way they are. He will leave and you will fall apart."

"Papa, I am so much stronger than that. I know you think I'm so young, such a child, so soft. But I'm tougher than you think."

He makes a clucking sound. "Irina? She is tough, hard to crack. You? You have always been softer, quieter, more delicate."

"You are too overprotective, Papa. I know who I am and what I can handle. I want to give this a shot, this thing with Tyler. And I want to finish the semester here. I want to stay. I like it here and I'm doing well, working hard."

"This semester was a trial. I will let you stay through the semester and I will stay, too. We will stay for the final games to see your brother play, and the playoffs. After you finish your classes, we will go home for the summer to sort things out. I do not want you seeing him, though. This is not negotiable."

"But—"

"No. This is for your own good. Tyler Lockhardt is not a part of your life, Zoya. If you want to stay here for your education, that is the rule."

I clamp down, tears overflowing again. It's not worth the argument. I've made my case, presented my truth, and he will not listen. My father is nothing if not resolute. I have rarely seen him change his mind about anything once a decision has been made. The fact that he will let me stay the rest of the semester, and also consider me coming back next semester is a huge concession in and of itself. Trying to convince him Tyler can be good for me, that he's worth getting to know, would be futile at this point.

My heart is heavy as my phone rings, Tyler's handsome face on the screen. I haven't texted him or called him since I left yesterday morning. It's been over twenty-four hours, and in that time, my heart has broken a million times. *He doesn't deserve my silence.* But the grief, the pain, the guilt of what Irina will feel, has taken my confidence. *This is not fair.* Even if Papa is right that I "disobeyed" him, this is not right. *Please forgive me, Ty. Please know I will do everything I can to get back to you.* Please know my heart is yours.

I hit "ignore," and let my tears flow freely.

28
drunk texting

Tyler

Six days later.

"**F**uck!" I yell, pulling off my helmet and throwing it to the ground in the bad box, where I will sit for the next two minutes, watching Portland probably take advantage of the power play. We're down one-two with seven minutes left to make up the two goals we need to win. It's not impossible, but our play hasn't been great tonight. It's not just me, the whole team is flat for some reason. Kolochev seems distracted. *Not really surprised there.* Bastard. Kazmeirowicz is just not hitting the mark, despite tons of shots on goal. It's a cluster, for sure, and my penalty box hat trick isn't helping.

I mean, I could blame it on the broken nose, but really, it's not that. I've left about ten messages for Zoya over the last days with no response. I know her dad is in town—I saw him talking to the coaching staff during pregame—so I figure he's just keeping a tight watch on her. I've stayed out of his line of sight, but I'm sure I can't avoid the guy forever. But Zoya... does she regret what we did? I sure as hell hope not as it was one of the best moments of my fucking life.

To make things worse, my mom was offered early release from jail as a plea deal, if she agreed to the one-year rehab out here. Her answer, according to James Blakney, the attorney, was, "Give me my goddamn kids back. You can shove that fancy rehab up your ass." So, not so much cooperation happening. Then she got in a fight with another prisoner and they leveled her with an assault charge that'll probably net her another six months, the possibility of any early release totally out the window. She won't see the outside of a cell for another two years minimum.

Fuck my life, you know?

This is too much fucking stress. I want my old life back, and... Oh shit! Evan just crossed to Mikhail and he scored!

Pay attention, shitbrain. Jesus. Get your motherfucking head in the game.

The clock winds down as I put my helmet back on, shooting out onto the ice as soon as the penalty clock hits zero. Back out there, I throw all my focus into defending the onslaught of shots on goal. There's this gangly Portland player who keeps baiting me to fight again but I don't bite. *Not gonna happen, dickbag.*

Three minutes left and Boris takes a quick pass from Viktor to the goal. This game is ours. An animated dragon huffs and breathes fire on the jumbotron—the Ice Dragon has proved once again just why we brought his ass here from Austin.

The arena is alive. Like, it's so loud I can hardly hear a damn thing happening in the game, and when it ends, fuck me, it's like my eardrums are gonna burst. I love it—and normally I'd be soaking it up and heading straight out to find some liquor and some hockey honeys to help me celebrate.

As it is, even with the high energy surrounding me, I just want to be alone. I feel like smashing something, punching something. No Bueno.

I toss my contacts in the trash as soon as I get into the locker room, half blind and thankful I have an excuse not to look anyone in the eye postgame. I shower, ignoring the loud celebration happening, my thoughts getting darker and darker.

Once I'm dressed, I pull on my glasses, hitch my bag over my shoulder, and walk out. No words for anyone. I just want to find a hole-in-the-wall somewhere where I can sit and nurse as many drinks as it'll take for me to black out.

Three drinks in and two women approach. "Hey, nice game tonight." I barely give them a glance. Mid-twenties, average looking. I just thank them and return focus back on my drinking.

Drink number four and I barely feel a damn thing. Fuck me, can't even get blackout drunk like I want. I get up to take a piss and another woman approaches. This one's hot, I guess. She's not a Zoya scale of hotness by any stretch of the imagination, though. Zoya, the gravitational force holding me in an endless orbit. Zoya, who won't call me back. Won't open my texts. I growl and punch the wall, not hard enough to do any damage, not with any real conviction.

"You okay?" the woman asks. "Want to go somewhere and talk it out?"

"Lady, I spent six minutes in the penalty box this game. You really want to hang out with me in this mood?"

She lifts a shoulder, flips her long, blonde hair over her shoulder. "Suit yourself."

Shaking my head, I do my business then head back out to my bar stool, ordering a fifth beer and a shot of tequila. Just as I shoot it back, I feel a hand on my shoulder.

"Fuck off," I yell, assuming it's yet another bimbo trying to get my attention.

It's not another bimbo.

Smokeshow is standing in front of my eyes, her beautiful face tight with worry, her soft floral scent instantly soothing. "Hey. Are you okay?" she asks.

Am I okay? My heart's about to leap out of my chest—at least, what's left of it after watching her get dragged out the door by her Cro-Magnon brother.

"What are you doing here?"

"What are *you* doing here? It looks like a pity party."

"Har har. I like the way you say 'pity party' in your Russian accent. Way hot, baby."

"Where are the kids?" She ignores my flirting.

I look around. "Nanny."

"Well, that's good, I suppose. They aren't sitting

around the apartment trying to fend for themselves. Does she know you planned to be out late?"

"Yes, yes. I'm not the biggest shitpole in the universe, you know. I told her I was going out to celebrate after the win. All is well."

"Well, you are in no state to go home, but you also don't look like you are *celebrating*." Zoya puts air quotes around the last word. "In fact, you look perfectly miserable."

"How did you find me in here?"

"You drunk texted me your location a few minutes ago."

"Whoa. I'm *drunk*?" I ask dramatically. "Been fuckin' tryin' all goddamn night!"

Zoya tries to hide a grin as she holds out her hand. "Come on, Ty. Let's get something in your stomach then find a place for you to sober up."

I take her hand and stand, suddenly wobbly. She helps me close out my tab before walking me outside into the evening. "How'd you get away from the Gestapo?" I ask as we make our way down the busy street.

"You are being stupid. The Gestapo were German. And also Nazis. My father is not a Nazi."

"Whatever," I say, rolling my eyes. "He isn't the boss of you."

"I'm here, right? I got your text and slipped away during our postgame dinner. My father has texted me so many times I had to turn off my phone."

"Such a rebel."

"Stop being a jerk. I came for you. Because I care for you. I want to be with *you*."

"Your family thinks I'm a piece of shit and you know what? They're probably right. I'm not good for you. You're sweet and innocent and I'm a big dummy. You should stay away from big dummies like me."

"Can you even hear yourself? You are so drunk right now, and you don't mean what you're even saying. Here's an Italian place. Can we get spaghetti or something? Tyler?"

I nod, suddenly very tired, and we head in, sitting at a tiny, tiny table that reminds me of a little kids' table, like one where the stuffed animals would have a tea party with plastic teacups. We order spaghetti with meatballs, a salad, and some bread, but pass on the red wine. The pitcher of iced water that arrives at the table suddenly feels like nectar from the gods. Zoya pours a tall glass for each of us and then clasps my hands across the table.

"I love you," she says simply.

I meet her eyes, golden-flecked brown and arresting, shining with tears. "Why the heck are you crying? Did I say other stupid shit to you other than the Gestapo thing?"

"You said you are no good for me, but I disagree. I think you *are* good for me."

"Why do you think that?"

"Because you make me happy, Ty. You make me laugh. You open up for me. I get to see the real you that other people don't get to understand. You have such a good heart and you work so hard. You're my friend. A true friend. And now, my lover. My first lover."

I swallow and try to look away but Zoya pulls one hand free and puts it on my cheek, forcing me to look back at her. "I'm a poor piece of trash from Southie. I'm just shit, Zoya. I happened to get lucky, find somethin' I was good at, but I'm nobody. Certainly not anybody your pedigree family would ever let mess with the bloodlines."

"Stop. Tyler. I love you. I mean it. This is not a game to me, and I'm not going to let you push me away because you think you have to live in this assigned space where people think you belong."

She's wrong. Take away my hockey stick and money, and I'm still a nobody.

"What did your dad say? Why haven't I heard from you in like a whole week?"

"He said you are the wild hockey player he does not want for his daughters. He says you will leave me in pieces."

Our food comes and we eat in silence. I admit, some sustenance does bring me slightly back to center. Slightly. I still feel buzzed as we eat, but while everything else has that fuzzy haze of inebriation, Zoya is crystal clear to me. Bright-eyed, pink-cheeked, gorgeousness. She's a fucking angel. *And she loves me.*

Has anyone ever said they loved me before?

Certainly not my ma. All she has done throughout my life has hurt me. Leave me gasping in anger and sadness.

"Do you think I'll leave you in pieces?" I'm

terrified I will. But I'm also terrified if she says that she's taken her father's words as gospel.

"No, Ty. I don't. I know I'm young, but I've been exposed to a great example of marriage from my parents. My dad can be a tyrant, and he can be an ass to my mother with his words at times. She calls him on it, of course. But seeing how they trust each other, how they treat each other...reverently. She feels safe with him, despite his temper, despite his overbearing nature. And, I feel the same with you, but without the overbearing nature of course."

"Wow. Okay." I don't know how to respond to that because the mention of marriage threw me right off. I have seen that same devotion in Georg's expression when he looks at his wife, though. And Viktor when he looks at Scarlett. *Adoration.* Big word to get out when you're drunk. And as I look into Zoya's beautiful eyes, all I can feel is *want.* "You want to go get a fancy hotel room and finish this conversation in private?" I ask after another moment of soaking her in.

She nods, biting her lip.

Thirty minutes later, we're inside a luxury suite at the Bellagio. I asked for a fountain view, so we could see the lights dance and change outside the window.

We stare out the window for a long time until I get the courage to say it back to her. "I—I love you, too." I've never said those three words to anyone, and although I wish I felt brave, I don't.

You're lucky you have me as your ma, son. No one

else would have ya. I've heard those words for years, so am I actually capable of love?

Still, we don't look at each other, though I feel Zoya clasp her hand in mine. Something about touching her sends electrical currents through my whole body. I feel alive when I'm touching her.

When I pull her body against mine, there is little restraint to be had. I'm still half-crocked and this is probably an awful idea, but I want her so badly.

And **she** *loves me.*

She **loves** *me.*

She loves **me**.

I'm a goddamn sap bastard but it's all I keep hearing in my head, over and over again, as my lips meet hers. Her mouth parts on a heavy sigh as my tongue pushes in deep and claims her mouth. *She loves me and she's mine.* One hand still holding hers, one on her neck I kiss the fuck out of her as her other hand finds my ass, boldly pushing my hips toward hers.

With a growl, I pick her up, her legs wrapping around me as I push her against the floor-to-ceiling window. I kiss at her mouth, her jawline, her ears, her neck. She sighs and moans and has her hands all over me, stroking over my cock and grinding against me until I feel like we might break the window with the force of whatever this is between us. Wild, unchained desire.

Still attached, I walk us over to the massive California king bed, where we fall into a giggling heap. Not romantic at all, but neither of us cares as we shed our clothing, tossing shoes and socks and shirts and underwear until there is nothing between us.

She pokes a finger at my glasses. "These are so, so sexy. Leave them on?"

I can't help but grin. "Nerdy."

"I love you nerdy."

"A nerdy fuckin' smokeshow, that's what you are," I say before kissing the tip of her adorable nose. "But now, I wanna lick your pussy until I feel you coming all over my face, okay?"

"Okay," she whispers, looking like a fucking feast laid out on this bed at the Bellagio waiting for me to do what I've promised.

Kissing my way down her body, I stop for an appetizer of two ripe, perfect tits, topped with hard, tightened nipples that I can't leave alone. I suck them into my mouth, releasing each one with a loud pop that makes Zoya arch and gasp each time I do it. I kiss her flat belly and tongue the ring piercing her bellybutton. I bite at her hipbones, and she moans in a way that makes my cock harder, if that's even possible.

Zoya looks down at me as I lick her from back to front, my tongue finding its way to her clit. Her head falls back on the bed as her mouth opens, a sigh escaping. It's all the encouragement I need as I suck that small bud onto my tongue, vibrating against it as my fingers find her wet, slippery pussy and bury two of my fingers inside her.

She's so responsive, her cunt tightening around my fingers as I work her into a frenzy. Hips rise off the bed, fingertips clutch desperately at the bedding, small desperate noises fall from her lips. I love it. Every movement, every noise. I love it all and I don't stop until she stops breathing, back arching, eyes closed as she rides a wave of orgasm that seems to last into eternity.

When it finally stops, she says, "Your turn."

"My turn for what?" I ask, crawling up beside her, kissing her cheek.

She pushes me to my back and climbs on top, splitting those long legs of hers over me as she repeats everything I just did. Sucking on my nipples, kissing my belly. She bites my hipbones and I laugh out loud.

But no one is laughing when she opens her mouth and takes a taste of my cock. I watch every second, the way she licks and sucks, her tongue sweeping across the head, down the shaft. When she takes me in, all the way down, and deep-throats me, I nearly come right then and there.

"Where did you learn such naughty things?" My voice is a desperate, needy rasp, and pointless because she doesn't answer. She just keeps doing it until I know I'm gonna come in her mouth. I can't stop myself and she won't stop sucking my cock, so it's gonna happen.

I think words or something spill out of my mouth when I start to come, holding her head in my hands as she takes me down, her beautiful eyes staring into mine. The intense eroticism in the moment between us is something I know I've never experienced with anyone else before this night with her. And one I can never forget.

When I can finally pull my cock out of her mouth, she swallows again and then licks her lips slowly, the wicked smile on her beautiful face teasing me mercilessly without ever uttering a single word.

I'm in shock.

This beautiful virgin, just deep-throated me, swallowed my cum, and then fucking smiled at me while she was licking her lips. What the fuck? How can she even be real?

And, she told me she loves me, too.

When I'm finally able to bring my brain back online, I pull her up on top of me again, our bodies aligned as I touch the smooth skin of her back, her ass, the backs of her thighs. We kiss some more, tasting ourselves on each other's tongues. It's maybe the sexiest thing I've ever done.

"I've never felt this before. Any of this with anyone else before you," I admit against her mouth. "I don't want you to change anything. I don't want to change you. I just wanna be with you...and love you. That's all I want, Zoya."

She answers by slipping on top of me, taking my cock deep inside her...where she's warm and wet and pulsing with desire.

Showing me how much she loves me too.

29

manning up

Zoya

T he water is hot and comforting. Tyler massages my back as I brace my hands against the cool tiles, simply enjoying every sensation.

"My legs feel—"

"Like jello," he finishes with a dark, amused chuckle. "Amazing sex can do that to a person."

"Was it? Amazing?"

"Was it not?"

I feel my cheeks heat. "For me, yes. I don't have much experience, though, so maybe not for you?"

His arms wrap around my waist, his front to my back as he nuzzles my neck. "You are perfect in every way and when I tell you it was amazing, you have to believe me."

I turn to face him, letting him wrap me in his big body's warmth. I love this, how we fit together. He makes me feel small and precious and protected, something difficult to find when you're tall.

"This feels so good with you—God, where have you been all my life?"

I kiss his chest, my hands snaking down to trail along his hard, muscled abs. "I'm here now, and I feel you too," I say, taking his heavy cock in my hand and holding him as he grows long and hard.

"Stop that or we're heading for round two, and I know you must be sore."

I don't stop, feeling bold as his cock twitches against my belly. I move one hand to stroke it, silky and long, as he rests his forehead against mine, his back arched like a cat as I pet him.

His mouth finds mine as he lifts me up, putting himself back inside me, plunging in and out as my back hits the tiles and my fingers find purchase against the skin of his back. He's been so gentle with me, so sweet and kind and caring. But now I don't want more gentleness from him. *I want him to fuck me.*

"Faster," I beg. "Fuck me harder."

He groans my name and answers my call, pumping harder and faster as the water sprays us both. His mouth is hard against mine, his kisses urgent, his tongue penetrating my mouth in tandem with his cock penetrating my sex. It's deliriously good. I never want him to stop.

We come together after a time, "I love you" on both of our lips like a sacred prayer.

TOWELING each other off after the epic shower sex —I'm certain I will remember for the rest of my life— I can tell that Ty has something on his mind. His whole demeanor has changed, and his mood has gone to serious. I am hesitant to even ask him what's wrong when he saves me the trouble.

"You should call your father."

"No. Why?"

He holds me by the arms and pleads his case, his steely blue eyes boring into me. "*I* need to take you to him, okay? I need to make him understand *this* —what we have together. I love you, Zo. I love you so much and all I want is to make you happy and for us to be together, but *he needs to believe that.*"

I bite my lip, on the verge of tears again. I'm afraid if he takes me to my father, I'll be on a plane by tomorrow morning. My time in Vegas will be over before Tyler can utter a word of explanation. I shake my head and wander away, trying to control my panic.

"It's the only way this will ever work, Zo. You know it and I know it. You're missing in action right now, and you're with me—the enemy—and I have to make this right with them." He's come up behind me, his chin resting on my shoulder, his lips finding my cheek and kissing me there, his beard stubble brushing against my skin.

Oh, God, how can I let him do this?

I cannot turn back to face him again. I cannot bear to witness the pain I know I'll see in his eyes of not feeling worthy of me to my family. I know he feels that way. He said it last night. *Your family thinks I'm a piece of shit and you know what? They're probably right. I'm not good for you. You're sweet and innocent and I'm a big dummy.* I don't want to face my father just yet, because I want to hold on to this precious time with him for longer.

But I can feel how insistent Ty is going to be on this matter, so I compromise. "If you must, I recommend you start with Pam. I'm not speaking to my brother right now, and I'm not really ready to go there with my father either. Maybe you call her and tell her I am fine and safe with you."

He gives my shoulder a squeeze before wrapping his towel around his waist and heading into the bedroom, dialing his phone.

"Hey, Pam," he says, putting her on speaker. "Just calling to check in."

"Hey there, troublemaker. Can I assume Miss Zoya is with you?"

"She is. She found me after the game. We're together and she's safe. But we need some help. We need to talk to the family, plead our case."

"Well, you'd be pleading it to a judge if not for Georg. Kirill was ready to have the police out looking for a kidnapped coed."

"Yeah," I breathe on an unamused laugh. "I'll bet he was," I say to Pam.

"What is going on, guys? This the real thing?"

"Yes," Tyler says into the speaker.

"Pam, we are in love. We want to give this a real try. I need Papa to understand that Tyler is a good man. That he loves me."

Pam considers this and takes a pause before finally saying, "I'll do my best to get folks together and ready to listen calmly. I can't promise it'll end up that way, but I'll do my damnedest, guys."

What my brother ever did to deserve Pam, I certainly don't know. I remember wondering about her parents when he first told us he had a girlfriend. Did they judge my brother by the same standard as they're judging Tyler now?

After we hang up with her, we have a tentative plan, but I'm still nervous as hell about the whole thing. I turn to Ty and realize it's time to plead *my* case. "You don't have to do this. You don't have to face him. I choose you. He will have to accept that or lose me."

"No, baby, no." He shakes his head slowly. "You have a family that loves you. They're crazy because they care about you. Don't give that up. I don't ever want that for you. I want him to respect me and know that I love you, and also that I respect him. I need to go talk to him."

I can see I am without any other options. Ty is correct even if it will hurt us in the end. It's already hurting us. I nod and rest my cheek on his strong chest as his arms wrap around me, holding me close.

"I still think this is a dumb idea, but I love that you want to do it. I'll go with you to talk to my father."

AFTER A FEW RESTLESS hours of sleep, we wake up at seven in the morning and prepare to set out for Pam and Georg's place, where we will all meet with my father and sister, who I've not seen or spoken to in one week. She was very hurt. Understandably so, but still it's another painful reminder of doing exactly what I promised *not* to do with Tyler and then lying about it.

The minute we get there, I regret it. Georg looks like he hasn't slept in days, his beard thicker than the five-o'clock shadow he usually rocks, his hair wild and untamed. He's in a white T-shirt and cargo shorts, his feet bare, his eyes barely open as he nurses a giant cup of steaming hot coffee. The two of us do not say a word to each other. Like I said, it will be a long time before I can forgive my brother for his betrayal.

Pam hands my father a mug, as well, but he just sets it on the table in front of him and crosses his arms, his lips a thin line, his eyes narrowing and laser focused on where Tyler's hand is clasped with mine.

"Papa," I say.

"Do not Papa me," he snaps. "I gave you an order. Do not see him. And what did you do? You snuck away like a petulant child. You ran away to find him and left us wondering if you were hurt!"

"Why would I be hurt?"

"It is a big city. You just disappeared. No call, no text. You could have been kidnapped. Raped. Killed."

"Well, I was not killed, clearly."

"Don't be smart mouth with me, daughter. This is serious."

"It's seriously an overreaction. I went to find Tyler and we spent the night together."

My father bangs his fist on the table. Georg seems to have finally found his words, saying, "Zoya, it really was very irresponsible to not leave us a message at least."

"I'm an adult and you all treat me like a child," I yell. "I'm not a child. You don't get to tell me who I can see and where I can go. I do nothing wrong. I study. I take school seriously. I will volunteer somewhere. These are good things and now I have someone I love and suddenly I'm out of line?"

"Well," Irina says, speaking from her seat on the couch, "You made me a promise and you broke it. Is that not out of line?"

"I am sorry, I truly am, Rina. I love you and you are my best friend. I tried to stay away from him. I went to tell him that nothing could happen, but it did because the feelings were already there. We love each other, Rina. I need you to be happy for me."

"Oh, well, if you're in love then..." She still won't look at us.

Tyler lets go of my hand and steps forward. "Mr. Kolochev," he says, "I am so sorry we've gone against your wishes. I'm sure Zoya has told you we started out as friends. This started in an innocent place, but our feelings grew. This isn't just about sex—not for her, obviously, and certainly not for me. I also know she's young. I get it. She's your baby. It seems sudden. All of it, and I understand. But our feelings are real, and I need you to know that I do respect her. I love her. I don't want anything other than your daughter's happiness."

"You are all over the Internet," my father says. "Drinking. Whoring. You play well but you fight a lot. You are the opposite of a man I would want for my daughter."

"Actually, Kirill"—Pam steps in—"Tyler *is* a good man with a good heart. He's a lot like Georg. He's passionate and wild, yes, but his heart is good. He took in his young brother and sister recently. He hasn't been out on the party scene in many months. He works hard on the ice. Georg changed…and Tyler can too. I believe he already has."

My father. stares at Pam, his chest rising and falling as he considers her words. "Pamela, I love you like a daughter. You were good for Georg. You helped him be a better man and I thank you for this. But Zoya is barely more than a child. She is too young, and she needs to step away from this drama and come home. She needs to grow up a bit. It is clear she was not ready to come here, to be so far away from her parents' influence."

Pam looks at Georg and they seem to have a couples-only conference before heading out of the room, back toward the bedrooms. A moment later, they come back, except this time Haley and Logan are holding their hands.

Tyler's face goes white. He falls to his knees as the kids skip over to hug him.

"Haley, Logan how'd you guys get here? Where's Patricia?"

"Georg and Pam gived her a break," Logan says proudly. "They buyed us donuts!" Tyler drops his head in defeat and just hugs the kids harder.

"We stopped at your apartment looking for you guys," Pam says. "Patricia said she wasn't expecting to stay all night, so we offered to take them with us, so they had a sleepover here."

"Oh, Christ," Ty says, running a hand nervously through his blond hair. "Georg, Pam...I'm so. I wasn't thinking...didn't think to... I need to call Patricia. I'm so sorry, to all of you." He looks absolutely devastated and broken. *I can't believe I didn't think to raise the question of the kids again once we left the bar. This is on me, too.*

There is a moment of quiet before my father stands. "Tyler, I see you have a lot going on in your life. Important things, and I can see you are growing as a man. But this is not a good time for romance. And my daughter will always come first for me. These kids should come first for you. I have made my decision. Zoya is coming home now."

He places his hand on my back as he nears, turning me toward the door, ushering me out into the hallway. He calls for Irina who, without her normal commentary, stands and follows us out.

I can't look back or I'll lose it. I know how badly Tyler must feel about leaving the kids with their nanny all night long. I can only imagine how heavy his heart must be.

The tears start the moment we get into a waiting town car.

They don't stop while I pack up my dorm room.

They don't stop as we head to the airport to put me on a plane back to Russia. Alone.

They don't stop until I finally fall asleep at thirty thousand feet.

30
playing with heart

Tyler

One month later.

It's playoff season. Las Vegas has hockey fever, the energy around our bid for the Cup intensifying with each win. They should rename it Crush Vegas, for the abundance of posters and billboards and news reports about us.

The marketing team has reintroduced the larger-than-life banners around the outside of the arena, each of us immortalized, three stories tall like hockey-playing kaiju. I should love it, should be basking in the glory of being a superstar among superstars, but really, I'm just a heartbroken kid.

I miss my girl. I miss her so much it aches and it's not about the sex. I miss her friendship most of all. I miss talking to the one woman who ever told me she loved me. I have the single text she sent me about an hour after her father marched her out the door. It's clipped like she was interrupted... My best guess? Dad killed her phone before he put her on the plane back to Saint Petersburg.

> Zoya: Ty...I love you. I'm so sorry...I won't stop loving you even though I am far away. Don't forget thaxociv,.

I won't forget. You. That you love me. I'll never *forget.*

So yeah... It hurts to imagine the scenario going down when she pressed send on that text.

I know she got on the plane alone though. Her dad stayed in town immediately after and Irina was still around for a while. I saw her at a home game sitting in VIP behind the bench. We didn't speak. I guess Dad wasn't successful in getting Irina to leave before her semester finished up. I agonize about Zoya's classes all the time. Did she get to complete them via distance learning? She must've been frantic having to just ditch the semester and the stats class she hated but worked so hard in. I know how much school means—*meant* to Zoya. My heart's just fuckin' broken. For her. For me.

And I take full blame.

I fucked up. And because I did, I wasted her semester on top of everything else.

Sorta like my whole life has been fucked.

I love you, too, Smokeshow. I'm so sorry, for everything. And I won't ever stop loving you even though you are far away...

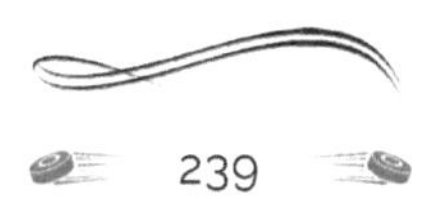

WE BEAT out Portland in the first five games of the playoff round. Coming off a late season win against them really messed up their mojo. The games weren't easy, per se, but Portland's fire was dimmed and ours was turned up extra hot. I put everything I had into those games; my focus laser sharp. To be honest, I had to, otherwise I'd have crapped out thinking about Zoya.

In between games, I've been trying to be a great role model for the kids. I still feel damn guilty about leaving them with the nanny the night I stayed at the Bellagio with Zoya. It was irresponsible, and I had to get down on my knees—literally—and beg Patricia not to quit afterward. She stayed, but only with a promise I'd be a model citizen.

We all board the bus from the Austin airport to the hotel and I go straight to the back, AirPods in to avoid having to interact with the other humans. Georg won't even look at me—it's a miracle we can play together right now. I think he wants to kill me and I'm not even exaggerating.

I adjust my glasses and pull out a book I've been reading about Buddhist philosophy—yeah, go figure. I know Zoya likes yoga, so I found a class to join and started going. I discovered right away that it really helped chill my anxiety. It's a gift, I tell you. Seriously, I think yoga might be my single saving grace these past weeks.

When a big lunk flops down beside me, I nearly snarl, then realize it's my team captain. Also, snarling is not very Zen, either. My yoga teacher would be disappointed in me. I pull out a pod. "'Sup, Evan?"

"Hey man, how's it going?"

I stare at him, unblinking. "Are you really just asking how things are going?"

He lifts his chin at my book. "Converting to Buddhism?"

"Converting would require some level of spirituality to begin with," I explain. "I have none, so I'm really just learning."

"That's...well...it's bloody surprising, frankly. But hey, I wanted to catch you for a minute before things get loud. You doing okay out there?"

"On the ice?" I ask, confused by his question. "I mean, yeah. I'm fine. Playing textbook defense lately. Laser focus and all that."

"I can see you're playing with focus, and I appreciate that, but I can't help but notice that you're not playing with any heart. You're there but you're not, you know what I mean? Normally you're up everyone's ass, pushing, fighting and I haven't seen that from you in weeks. What's going on?"

I give him a weird bark of a laugh and a shake of the head. "Ask your best friend what's going on."

Evan's eyebrows shoot up into his forehead. "Georg?" Then, realization dawns on him. "Oh. His sister."

I nod. "I mean, it's not his fault, I guess. He's just the enforcer."

"You really cared for her?"

"Fuck." I blow out a big breath. "I know it's hard

to believe but I did. *I do.* You said I'm not playin' with heart? It's probably because I got my heart ripped out when she was dragged back to Russia."

Evan's lips push to one side, a crease forming between his eyes. "Interesting. Well, I'm sorry, man. It's a shit break, but I can only advise that if something's meant to be, it'll be. Love manages to find a way, you know?"

"I guess."

"We need you out there, Locksey. All of you."

"Got it, chief." I put my AirPods back in, but he doesn't leave. He looks off into the distance, then nudges me with his elbow. I pull out the pod again. "Yeah?"

"I never saw myself falling in love. Not until I met Holly. She just...I don't know. Knocked me on my arse, I guess. I had to try really fucking hard, you know? And she tried just as hard not to let it happen. But we found a way and I feel more like a man now, married with children, than I ever did when I was fucking my way through the city. So, I get how it can gut you when you find it."

I stare at him, blinking, trying to figure out what to say. Evan and I get along fine but we're not buddies. We don't talk like this. I open my mouth a couple of times and shut it again. Finally, I just settle for, "Thanks."

He nods, sits for a second, then stands up, heading back up to the front of the bus.

I think I must read the same line in my book fourteen times by the time we pull up to the hotel. I check in, making sure I'm set up with an adjoining room for Patricia, who's flying in with the kids so they can watch the game.

When they arrive, they're like little tornados of kid energy, jumping on the bed, asking for room service, ordering me to take them to the pool. We head down in our bathing suits and flip-flops, big beach towels around our necks, the kids each holding one of my hands. And even though I feel so brokenhearted, I don't think I would have survived the past month without these two. Their daily smiles and cuddles, which took a while to earn, their stories about new friends from school. Their bright presence in my otherwise solitary life. I look down at their little, trusting hands, and can see so much change in them. They look healthier and stronger, and as they chatter about their plane trip and the nice "hostesses", I smile. I've set up a spa treatment for Patricia, who really is a fucking miracle of a human, so she's got tonight off.

Pam and Georg are at the pool when we get down there, jumping in to play an epic game of Marco Polo with me and the kids. Well, Haley has a go, mostly dogpaddling, since Ma never taught the kids to swim... surprise, surprise. Patricia's been taking the kids to swimming lessons since she started, so Haley isn't bad. Logan spends most of the time on my back in a monkey grip, meaning we didn't go under the water. And even though things are awkward and uncomfortable between Georg and me, I've caught him smiling and laughing at Logan. The kid *is* cute.

I want—badly—to ask about Zoya, but something about the way Georg carries himself around me makes me think it's not a good idea. It makes me sick to my stomach, not knowing. Not being able to talk to her. Either way, I haven't heard from her since her lone text message on the last day that I saw her. She's like a princess locked away in a tower or something. And we've already established that I'm no Disney prince, so…yeah, the situation sucks severely.

After the pool, we all go out for dinner and a movie, which I yawn all the way through. As we're walking out of the theater, Logan is conked out draped over my shoulder. Pam pulls me back when Georg takes Haley to play a couple of video games.

"You okay, bud?"

I lift a shoulder. "Tired. Haven't been sleepin' well."

"Because of the thing with Zoya?"

"Ya think?" I immediately feel like a dick for my tone. She's just trying to be nice and I shouldn't be an asshole to a friend. "Sorry, Pam, I am complete and utter shit for company these days, but yeah, it's Zoya, but also my mom, too. She agreed to the rehab when she realized it was gonna be two years in jail otherwise, but she's been calling at all hours, bitching me out, askin' for cigarettes or money or whatever nonsense. She wants me to get a lawyer to get her out early. It's a fuckin' nightmare and I don't really—" I stop talking and stare at her.

"Zoya was right. You don't really have anyone to talk to about it because… she's not here."

"Wow. You're readin' minds now, Pam."

"Yours is pretty easy to read. And I feel heartbroken for you, for what it's worth."

"It's not even just being heartbroken over not having the woman I love with me, you know? I feel… overwhelmed. Exhausted. This is a lot. And I know everyone says I'm doing this good thing for the kids and I'm tryin' my best, but I'm just fuckin' exhausted, you know?"

Pam pulls me and Logan into an awkward hug. One arm hangs limp at my side as she holds me close, but I rest my chin on her shoulder. I'm beyond being comforted at this point. I feel empty and tired and I just wanna sleep for a long fuckin' time.

I try to explain, "I appreciate you, I do. I'm just—"

"I get it, Tyler," she says, pulling away. "How about Georg and I take the kids for breakfast in the morning? Give you some time to sleep in?"

"That'd be awesome. Thanks."

AFTER WINNING game one in Austin, the team heads home to get ready for game two of the matchup. It's frenetic, and even in my depressed state, I feel the love from our city. My city. Vegas has become home for me in just a few short years and it's one of the only things keeping me afloat right now.

We play a tight, hard game two at home, winning one-zero, barely holding Austin off as they try to make paybacks for stealing the Ice Dragon away. He's a machine out there, battling for every shot on goal, managing to push one into the net for the win.

Then we're back on the road to Austin again, trying to sweep another round. Patricia stayed home with the kids, so I'm solo this trip. They only travel with me when the trip doesn't interfere with their school days. I'm serious about Haley and Logan having the structure of school and routine daily living. They've never had any normalcy before they came to live with me, so the least I can do for them is be consistent. Adhering to a schedule is not that difficult. You just have to commit to it.

So, I'm in the hotel bar on our first night back in Austin, nursing a beer when Georg meanders up and plops down on the stool beside me.

Unexpected choice of seating for him, but whatever.

He orders a seltzer water with lime and sits, twirling the straw between his fingers, not saying anything for the longest time.

"You're playing well," he finally says.

"You too."

A few more moments pass. "Okay, I'm just gonna say this and then I am done. Tyler, I feel like an enormous tool. I see how torn up you are, and we need to talk this out. I'm protective of my sisters, as you know. Probably because I knew how I was with women." He laughs darkly. "I was a real fuck, you know?"

"You're still a fuck."

"Sometimes. I guess I am. But in this particular

case, all I saw was my innocent baby sister half naked with a guy who I've witnessed—with my own eyes—fuck his way through countless bunnies over the last three seasons with the Crush, and saying he'll never be in a relationship."

"Fair enough. But in this particular case, all I saw was you flying off the fucking handle and breaking my nose before we could have an adult discussion about feelings."

"I'm sorry I broke your nose. And I'm sorry I couldn't see it. Didn't see it. I see it now, though. She loves you. You love her."

"I do love her. Though I don't know what she feels right now because I can't fuckin' *TALK* to her," I bite back at him, my volume far louder than it should be for being in a public bar.

"I'll see what I can do about that," he says after my outburst.

"Oooh. Gonna slip me her new number or something?"

He shakes his head at me. "Look, Tyler, I want you both to be happy. I really do. I know we've never been friends or whatever, but it doesn't mean I want you miserable and broken."

"Okay. Thanks, I guess?"

"If it helps, Zoya still hasn't forgiven me for outing her to our father. She's making me pay hard for not having her back about her relationship with you. She calls me *predatel'* now...her betrayer."

I can't help the sense of satisfaction that comes with hearing this news. My head goes up and down a few times. "Sounds about right. She is a Zen master after all. Zoya always speaks true." When he doesn't leave the bar, but keeps his ass planted on the stool, staring, I have to ask, "Something else on your mind, Georg?"

Georg bites his upper lip. "There is. Something else, I mean. Pam and I both want to talk to you. Can we get a table?"

I feel my brows furrow but nod, closing out my tab as we head to a table, Georg texting Pam to come down. She joins us and we order some appetizers, but I still have no clue why we're sitting here. Frankly, I was happier looking into the bottom of my beer bottle.

"Hey, just want to say thanks for your help with Haley and Logan. Appreciate it. It's hard, ya know? Livin' far from their home. But, they're happy here. I think. They really love you guys and talk about you all the time. Pretty sure Logan thinks Georg walks on water."

"Funny you should mention them," Pam says. "That's what we wanted to talk to you about."

I raise an eyebrow in question.

"We love Haley and Logan too," she says. "We really connect with them. It's weird, funny, how much, really."

"We never wanted kids," Georg adds. "Since we got together, babies have never been anything we've been interested in. Partly because we both fear them, but I've also had doubts about whether I could be a good enough dad to raise up another human without screwing them up."

I make a *meh* noise. "You're doing good. A helluva lot better than me. You'd make a fine dad, I think."

"Well..." Georg clears his throat.

"We want to adopt Logan and Haley," Pam blurts.

I swear I nearly choke on my beer. "What?"

"Well, we don't know how it all works, of course. Maybe we foster them first? Then adopt? We just—we truly believe they're great and well, we want them in our lives."

31
kind of pregnant?

Zoya

Three weeks later.

Who would have guessed that I'd ever become a Crush junkie?

It's true. I even watch the games.

I've been streaming every single Crush playoff game online because I hope to see glimpses of Tyler. I pray for locker room interviews that feature him so I can hear his voice. I watch his old interviews on YouTube constantly. I still stalk his social media, but all his accounts went silent. Not a single new post on any of them. The games have been fun to watch, though I would never, ever admit it to my father. I thought Papa planned to stay in the US through the end of the season, but after everything that went down with Tyler, and after he put me on a plane back to Russia, he changed his mind and returned home with Irina as soon as her semester finished a few weeks later. Gratefully I was able to do finals and submit my final projects online. I got credit for all my units at UNLV, including STAT 152. The (A-) was a surprise. I won't have to take it again, but even thinking about stats now just wrecks me. Because of Tyler.

These have been the hardest seven weeks of my life.

I know I love Tyler, but in this time of silence, of not knowing, of feeling as though part of me is missing...I've never known such a sense of loss. Irina has forgiven me, especially after finding me sobbing one night about a week after she came home. She couldn't stay angry at me after that, and when she thought about it, she apologized to me, saying she'd been prideful and selfish to ask me to not sleep with him. That certainly helped, having my best friend—my sister—back again.

It still breaks my heart seeing Tyler, though, and when the cameras get near enough to show his face up close, his eyes look dead. The fire I know he has, is missing, even though he plays well. Normally, I think he fights a lot, ends up in the penalty box often. Lately my Ty has played a strong defensive game, but even I can see he is playing with no emotion.

The team is within reach of the Cup, heading into the finals, when my father calls us all together to FaceTime with Georg after game one. Mama, out at the shops, will be sorry she missed his call.

"*Pozdravlyayu!*" Papa says as Georg's face fills the

screen. "Three more games and you are a champion again!"

"The team is a champion," Georg says, pushing a hand through his hair. "It's been a bloody good season for us all."

"All except that *mudak*," my father mutters.

"Ah, well, that *mudak* is actually playing exceptional defense out there, as you well know, Papa. He is one of the best. You cannot deny. So it's his championship, too," Georg reminds him.

They are talking about Tyler, of course. My father never met a grudge he could not keep for a century. I roll my eyes and grit my teeth. I would give anything to talk to Tyler, but my father continues to remind me how it will never happen under his watchful eye. I have to respect Papa's wishes for now, but once this season is over?

Who knows...

Maybe I take a summer trip to Las Vegas or maybe Tyler takes a summer trip to Saint Petersburg. Something will change soon; I can feel it. I don't know how I *know* this, but I do.

"Well, we actually called to share some other news," Georg says. He pulls the phone away and Pam appears beside him.

"*Beremennaya?*" Irina asks.

"No," Georg says. "But kind of?"

"How can you be *kind of* pregnant?" I ask, suddenly re-engaged in the conversation.

"We're working with Tyler's attorney and

caseworker in Boston to get custody of Haley and Logan," Pam announces excitedly.

Kirill Kolochev is speechless. Irina is speechless. I am the first to recover. "You're adopting them?"

"Starting with fostering," Pam says. "We'll have to go through some legal hoops for a while to prove we're serious, but the end-game is adoption, yes."

"His mother will go along with this?"

"She's in a long-term rehabilitation center now, but it's not going well," Pam explains. "It's likely she'll go back to jail in Boston. James and Winter Blakney, the couple we met on our honeymoon at Fripp Island, are handling the case for us in Boston. You met them when you were all there with us. Anyway, James says there's plenty of grounds to permanently restrict her access to them. And Winter feels like no judge would overlook an opportunity to put two neglected, abused kids into a better permanent home."

"Wow." It takes me a minute to absorb her words. "I do remember James and Winter from Fripp Island. How wonderful you have experts to help you with this process. It's amazing. Really. And surprising, I guess? I thought you didn't want to ever have children?"

Georg gives an impish grin. "Well, technically, we didn't have children."

"Be serious, *predatel'.*"

"I am being serious. We didn't have children, we found them. They found us. And while we certainly enjoy the act required to make babies, we do not actually want babies. But older kids? And these two…

Haley and Logan? Well, we love them both very much. They fit with us, and we fit with them."

I nearly cry thinking about this news. "Tyler must be very relieved," I say. "He was so worried about a long-term solution."

"He was shocked, to say the least, but he's on board for sure. He can still be close by and part of their daily lives, but it takes the pressure off him, which is best for him and the kids. Relieved is a good word for it, I think," Pam answers thoughtfully.

"He's still troubled, of course, about other things," Georg adds.

I frown, looking at my father, who still hasn't said anything. Irina says, "Wow, congrats," then nudges Papa.

He makes a strange noise before saying, "I will be grandfather?"

They all talk for a few minutes when my brother asks for a moment to talk with Papa alone. He walks off with the phone, shutting himself in his office. The conversation switches to Russian.

About half an hour later, Papa emerges, red-faced.

"Must have been an intense conversation," Irina mutters, looking down at her book.

"Zoya," he says, ignoring my sister, "your brother has appealed on behalf of his teammate."

"Tyler, Papa, his name is Tyler. He is not Lord Voldemort. You can say his name."

He clears his throat. "Tyler." He grimaces. "Georg said he is convinced Tyler is now a better man; he has changed, and that he has earned the right to see you."

"I could have told you this a long time ago, Papa."

"Please do not—just—I am going against my better judgment. It is hard for me to see you growing up, to see you becoming a woman. You are the baby of this family."

"Papa, I may be the baby of this family, but I'm not a baby anymore. I'm a grown woman, an adult, and if anything, this last seven weeks has shown me how much I do love Tyler Lockhardt." I've felt heartbroken with an indescribable loss, which is crazy for how long we'd actually spent together. But I missed his conversation, his cheekiness, his strength. I miss him so much. "It is real—for both of us—and I can see how this is hurting him as it is hurting me. I can tell the difference between men who want only one thing and good men, and my Ty is a good man."

We meet each other's eyes for a long heartbeat before my father says, "If you really love him, then you should be together. You may go to be with the one you love, my Zoya."

After hugging my father so hard I worry I might have broken him, I can't get on a plane fast enough.

32
his blessing

Tyler

"Good to see some light in your eyes, Locksey," Evan says, slapping me on the back as we head out to the tunnel. "Let's go win another fuckin' Cup for Vegas, yeah?"

"Chief." I tip my head at him. "Yeah, we got this." Slipping my mouth guard in, I pull my helmet down, and tighten the strap. As per usual, there are good-luck messages playing on the screens along the tunnel, well wishes from our loved ones as we head into the final.

I wait in line, knowing it'll be yet another year where I walk right by those screens. I've never had a single message from anyone—pathetic, right? Still, it's kind of fun to see a bunch of big-ass pro players get weepy when they see their moms or their girlfriends or wives on screen on the biggest night of their careers.

The whole day has been a big spectacle. We came in early, all in our monkey suits, to do pregame press and activities. There were marching bands and circus acts and all kinds of craziness outside the arena all day long. Right now, a big pop star is performing on the ice. Once she clears off, we'll go out for the pregame warmup. All these delays have me a bit jittery. I take some deep breaths and concentrate on relaxing with some techniques I learned from reading and my yoga instructor.

I recall the time when dumbass Kolochev had his big moment at the last home final we played here. Pam proposed to him in a Playboy bunny costume. Ridiculous.

Evan steps up to the screens and sees Holly and their kids wishing him good luck. He blows their images a kiss and heads on up. I start to walk by, but Scarlett stops me, grabbing my forearm. She motions to the screen, and there are Haley and Logan. Two bright-eyed little faces, telling me how much they love me and how much they loved staying with me, and how they'll be cheering me on from the stands.

My mouth is surely hanging open. I turn to Scarlett and she just grins and shoves me forward. A big-ass, dopey smile spreads across my face as I take the ice, waving at the crowd as I'm announced as a starter. Yes, I feel lighter knowing my brother and sister will have a loving home with two parents who genuinely love them and that I can be an active part of their life, too. I feel good about this plan with Pam and Georg, and it infuses me with a happiness I haven't felt in many weeks.

Not since Zoya left.

AFTER THE ANTHEM, we take our positions for the first period. We're playing Philly, who came back from a piss-poor start of the season as a dark horse for the Cup. They've been playing balls-out, with tight formations and a few trick plays that have caused us the losses leading to this seventh game.

The first minute is just chaos. Philly's center wings it back to a defenseman, who sends it to the wings, who sends it all the way across the ice, a sharp pass to the center again, who sends it flying at our goalie. Bam, bam, bam. I can hardly keep track of the puck, it moves so fast.

I'm on left back, supporting Mikhail, who manages to get a dagger shot on goal that nearly tips into the net out of their goalie's glove. The mostly Vegas-supportive crowd lets out a collective "Oh!" as the frenzied play continues.

With one minute to go in the first period, we're on a power play, with their left wing in the sin bin for punching Evan in the back after a check against the glass. It looks, for a second, like Boris will score from the center, but at the last instant, one of their defenders sweeps him off his feet, disappears with the puck, and shoots, scoring.

Boris is on his feet, arguing with the refs as the crowd breaks out in a chorus of boos. When the buzzer sounds, he comes off the ice wearing a scowl so sharp it could cut someone.

Coach is not happy. "How the fuck did we let

them score on our fucking power play?" he shouts. "Someone explain it to me, because it makes no motherfucking sense!"

Evan huddles us together. "Ladies. They are here to win. They've showed up for every game and they're showing up now. If we don't match their speed in the neutral zone, we're sunk. We look like a bunch of elephants lumbering around out there. Pick it up. Get on the forecheck. Look for the openings. You, defensemen, anticipate their offensive gaps. Tighten that shit up!"

The second period goes slightly better. We outshoot them three-to-one, but their goalie is on his mark every time. He doesn't let a single thing slide through. It's like he's glued to the net. To our credit, we don't let a single shot through, either, but it takes me, Georg, and Viktor all on our top game to stop the shots, which seem to be coming from every angle.

As we huddle again to start the third period, I can barely see from the sweat rolling into my eyes. Everyone looks fuckin' beat-tired and ready to die. We get a good pep talk from Coach Brown, and Evan says he'll buy everyone a pony if they can pull out two goals this period. Two goals and we're golden. We've done it before; we can do it again.

Coach has made hardly any substitutions all game. The starting lineup has probably played all but six or seven shifts of this game. He asks if we're good and we all give gloved thumbs up signals before hitting the ice for one last period.

Shortly after the period starts, Boris gets full-on

body-checked into the glass, so hard that his helmet flies off. He turns and pushes the defender, who punches him in the mouth. Viktor, Boris's enforcer, steps into the fray, a torrent of Russian swears coming out of both their mouths. And Boris doesn't swear, so…

Boris spits blood onto the ice and the crowd roars for retribution. I think I see a tooth, too, but I can't get past the melee. It takes several minutes to settle everyone down and clean up the equipment from the yard sale with several players going into the penalty box. Boris skates off with the medic. He's animated as he talks, then he tilts his head back and yep, there's a missing Chiclet.

Hey, it happens in hockey. I'm sure his hot-nerd girlfriend will have something to say about it later.

Snickering, because lost teeth are always amusing to me, I go back into position. Vik's in the sin bin, so they've sent out second-string rookie, Nathan Cross. Quiet, kind of weird in my opinion, he's superfast but not strategic. In practice I hear the defensive coaching staff constantly telling him to pass to someone, not just dump the puck into open space.

Georg is to his right, always at his best friend's back. I yell, "Hey, Kolochev, you gonna pull a surprise biscuit out of your ass like you did last year?"

"Better," he says. "No one else is getting a goddamn thing done out here."

To Cross, I say, "Stay here around the crease and support your goalie. That's it. Keep those shots outta that fuckin' net. Got it?"

He nods.

"Don't fuck this up, rookie, or I'll put fire ants in your boots," Georg says.

Play starts again and Cross, to his credit, does what he's told. He stays planted, blocking off players left and right as Georg and I try to move up a bit, to give more support to the wings. With our sniper, the Ice Dragon, out for a few minutes, we've got another second-string offensive player at center. Emile Giroux from Quebec—he's played lots of minutes, especially when Evan was out on IR for a bit. I like him but he's a bit of a loner. Georg says it's because he has a "French stick up his ass," but Vik thinks it's more that he's got anxiety or some shit.

Welcome to the club, dude.

Philly's line is changed up, too, with two of their players in the box, and I can see they're watching Giroux in the middle. Action picks up and I'm just analyzing their movements, their crutch-plays. Giroux is a strong passer, not a strong scorer, so every time he gets the puck, he fakes, pivots, and sends it sharply on to someone else. It gets predictable; I see three missed opportunities for a shot on goal.

We take a commercial break and I see Evan skate up to Emile and whisper to him. I don't know what he's saying but I'd wager money he's telling him to take a motherfucking shot.

When play starts again, two minutes later, he does just that. It pings off the left pole and lands right in front of Mikhail, who strikes it back to me. I send it to Evan, totally open on the right wing, and he sends a one-timer high, hard, and fast, right into the net while the goalie still has his eyes on me.

The crowd goes crazy. The ice feels like it's bouncing beneath my skates, and people are on their feet and screaming. Evan raises his stick high in the air, as we circle around him in celebration. Georg yells, "Fuck, yes! That's my bae!"

"That's one. Now do it again," Mikhail yells.

We set up with three minutes left and a tied game. The crowd is so fucking loud, it's insane. I rap my knuckles against my helmet, a reminder to stay focused, as the play starts up again. The puck starts moving our way, Georg deflecting a shot back to Evan, who passes to Giroux, who takes a shot. It gets deflected, Mikhail there to try to tip it in. As Evan skates up for support, there's a skirmish, sticks jabbing at the puck but not getting it out off the boards behind the net and back into play. I can hardly see what's happening until the crowd goes crazy.

"What just happened?" Cross asks.

I lift my shoulders because I sure as shit don't know, but the refs are calling it a goal.

"Greasy goal," Georg says, skating our way to embrace us all again. "Evan tipped it up over off the goalie's back into the net during the skirmish."

Philly requests a video review, but the goal is confirmed. We're up two-one with thirty seconds left. A few quick swipes, along with the crowd counting down, getting louder with every second—and the buzzer sounds, along with the decibel level in the arena. We're all screaming and yelling and jumping on each other as confetti drops from the ceiling and music plays and people cheer. We're all over the jumbotron, a bunch of sweaty-ass dudes, happy as shit to have won the Cup on pretty much the worst-ever goal in history.

People start pouring onto the ice as they bring out a rug, then a table, then the glorious Cup itself. People pass us hats with champion status imprinted on them. Flowers sail through the air and onto the ice. It's fucking chaos. Good chaos, but chaos, nonetheless. I see Logan and Haley way up in the owner's box with Pam, waving wildly, and I wave back. The whole thing is surreal.

As we line up for the presentation of the Cup, I look out and see many of the guys' family and friends and loved ones on the ice, phones out to capture the moment. Behind the first two rows of people, I notice a dark head of hair popping up, trying to see over the crowd, and my heart soars with hope. I know that head of hair. *Smokeshow.* Back in Vegas? Can she really be here? My heart, which spent nearly the last two months comatose and aching, wakes the fuck up in about two-point-five seconds, and practically leaps from my body to go to her.

The commissioner is talking and it's still hella loud, the energy level only slightly less what it was right after the win. I can't hear him at all, but I can see her clearly now. My beautiful, gorgeous, legs-for-days Zoya in jeans and boots and wearing a Crush jersey— with my number on it. All I can do is soak her up as I watch her weaving her way through the crowd, trying to get to the front. When she gets there, I think my face might split in half, I'm smiling so hard.

Georg elbows me and points, saying, "It's Zoya."

As if I wasn't already aware of the woman I love now standing mere feet away from me.

The commissioner presents the Cup to the team, but I couldn't give a shit at this point. I smile for a couple of pictures, but the person my eyes are devouring is the prize that really matters.

They start passing the Cup. First to Evan as team captain, and then it will go to each and every player in turn to have their individual moment holding the Cup and skating around the ice with it. It'll take a solid half-hour to get through the entire roster, and I'm not waiting thirty fuckin' minutes to go to my girl. This, I do know.

So, the minute I think it's okay, I skate over and pull her into my arms, kissing her cheeks, her hair, her lips. Never stopping, just taking her in as much as it's possible to do on national television broadcasting around the world...if the camera decides to land on us that is. We have to keep it G-rated.

"You're really here," I say against her sweet, soft lips.

"I'm really here, Ty."

We hold each other for a long time. When I pull away to look into the eyes I've missed so desperately over seven long weeks, I grimace. "I'm sorry, I probably smell like the inside of a camel's ass, but you smell divine as usual."

"A…camel's…ass?" she asks before bursting into a fit of giggles.

"Whatever. I'm wicked stinky. But I'm so happy now that you're here. Did you run away or somethin', Smokeshow?"

Zoya's eyes are filled with happy tears as she brings her hand up to cup my face, effectively freezing me in place, as only her touch can do and has ever done. If she's touching me, I don't want to move.

"No, I am here for you. My father has given his blessing and I am here to stay."

33
a good fit

Zoya

Hours later.

I bite the inside of my lip as we step into Ty's apartment, feeling suddenly very nervous. We haven't had really any private time together since our meeting on the ice. So much celebrating and so many traditions to carry out after winning the most sacred prize in all of hockey, the Stanley Cup. We've been out with everyone, had a million pictures taken, and seen the Vegas Strip explode in Crush colored lights. The whole city is one giant party right now that probably won't stop for at least a week.

But now our moment alone has come.

What if it's not the same between us? It's been weeks and we haven't even spoken. Maybe his feelings have changed? Maybe now that he doesn't have the kids living with him, he wants to go back to his old life. It was simpler, I suppose, in many ways. And yet, when I think of his face when he saw me on the ice—the raw happiness—I cannot doubt his feelings. How I've missed this man.

He flips on a lamp, filling the darkness with warm light that makes his blond hair shine like a halo.

Tyler. My Ty. He has his glasses on, black frames that make him look studious, serious. Until I read his T-shirt, which says, *If hockey was easy they'd call it soccer.*

"That shirt is stupid," I say, pointing at it.

He looks down and shrugs. "Meh."

"I mean it. Take it off."

He makes a face before his mouth forms an oh. "You want me to take my shirt off?"

"I do. I really do."

"No big talk? No catch-up?"

"We can talk while you take your shirt off."

Tyler grins. "Okay. You're the boss. Also, you're bossy."

"We've wasted so much time, and I don't want to waste another minute."

When he pulls his shirt over his head, I reach out to trace the lines of his tattoos with my fingertips as he shivers.

"Fuck, I've missed you," he growls, pulling me to him, his lips finding mine in a searing, hot kiss that has the power to make my toes curl.

He lifts me up and suddenly I'm on the dining room table as he kisses my breasts through my Crush jersey. My nipples ache against my lace bra—one I bought especially for seeing him again. He pulls the bottom of my shirt up, kissing my belly as heat pools between my legs.

I touch every panel of his stomach, the curves of his defined pecs. He's a machine, well-honed and at the top of his game. I can't believe he's mine.

"You are mine, right?"

His head pops up, a question in his eyes. "Did you mean to ask that out loud?"

"Yes and no," I answer.

His laugh is light. "Yes, I'm yours, baby. For however long you want me."

"Oh. Good."

A lopsided grin, and then, "Oh good?"

I push my lips together to keep from smiling. Ty makes his way up to kiss me, forcing me to let go. I kiss him back, still smiling. "I am so in love with you. I was worried you might have changed how you felt about me."

"Never." His accent makes it sound like *nevah* and I swoon at the sound. "I missed you every minute of every day. You ruined me for anyone else. All I see is you."

He picks me up and takes me to the bedroom, where we spend long minutes undressing each other. When I'm down to just my lace bra and thong, Ty has me stand so he can look at me. His gaze is dark and powerful as he stalks in a circle around me, his finger caressing the most sensitive skin of my backside, the sides of my stomach, the inside of my forearms. I break into gooseflesh.

"You are the most beautiful woman I have ever

known, hands down. But you are so much more than that to me. I know I'm a rookie when it comes to love and relationships, but I'm here for this with you, Smokeshow."

"Me too," I say, suddenly feeling shy.

"I love you." His voice is husky; he's so hard beneath his boxer briefs. *Hard for me.*

I reach out, licking my lips, my eyes on his as my hand finds its way beneath the cotton to find his hard cock, the silky skin of him filling my hand. He pushes my thong aside and slips his finger inside me, finding me ridiculously wet and wanting.

We kiss, just touching each other for so long that it almost feels dreamlike. It's quiet in here, and the only sounds are our soft sighs and moans and kisses.

I feel the buildup and I want to come so badly. I want him to feel me come, but not on his fingers. "I'm ready," I breathe. "Make love to me?"

Tyler slowly moves us toward the bed, where he removes the last two items of my clothing from my body, staring at my nakedness, taking his fill of looking. It only makes me hotter for him the way his eyes darken like a hungry wolf about to pounce.

His shorts are last before we are both fully naked, only the evening lights of Vegas illuminating us through the window. We fall onto the bed in a jumble of limbs, Tyler positioning himself on top of me, his lips never leaving mine.

When he pushes inside me, it's a tight fit. It hurts a little, at first, but then I breathe as he fills me all the way. I'm full of him, and it feels so right and perfect.

He kisses me deeply as he starts to move, gradually, taking slow strokes, filling me up and retreating, whispering words telling me how much he loves me, how beautiful I am. I let myself go and float along on the ride of Tyler making love to me. It's a ride I hope never comes to an end.

It's so good but I am ready for more. When I whisper to him my request, he hears me. Then he pulls my legs up to his shoulders and suddenly, he is so deep. So deep, it nearly takes my breath away. He goes into another mode of constrained wildness. I love it.

I wrap my arms around his back as he pushes in and out and in and out, in long, hard thrusts, in a delicious rhythm that hits against every sensitive part of me until I feel the start of the tingling, out-of-body orgasm that will crash through my body with a powerful wave.

I cry out, lost in a haze of pleasure and his kisses, climaxing again and again like it will never stop. On a wave that will carry me forever. I feel like I'm floating somewhere in the outer reaches of space but safe and protected and loved.

Only when it subsides does he let himself go, thrusting so incredibly deep when he fills me up with his release, groaning out my name on every hard thrust and jet of his cock spilling deep, deep inside me. I feel tears trailing from my eyes. And then I feel his lips kissing them away with more whispered words about how falling in love with me was the best thing to ever happen to him in his whole life.

We lie together for a long time, catching our breath, my head on his chest, his hand caressing over my body wherever he can reach.

"This feels like home," I whisper. "Being here with you. It felt like home the minute I walked in."

"It's not the place, it's the person," he says, kissing my head. "*You* feel like home to me. I want you here with me all the time. I need you, Zo. Since that first day at the tattoo shop. And I know you have a lot of life to live. You have school and goals and I don't want to get in your way at all. I need to make that clear."

He's so serious, it makes me giggle. "I hear you and I appreciate you supporting my goals. I want to finish school, too, but I want to do it with my best friend at my side."

"I'm still your best friend?"

"My best friend. My love. I don't care about the label. I only care about you."

"Well, I kind of care about the label. I mean, can I officially say you're my girlfriend without some Kolochev tryin' to take my head off?"

"You can. All Kolochevs are supportive. Even Irina, who is now sleeping with some guy who works at a coffee bar and has a man-bun."

"That sounds like a better fit."

"We are a good fit."

"We are. I can't believe I ever found you."

"You were looking?" Then I laugh and shake my head. "No, you were not looking."

"I wasn't, you're right. But now that I *have* you, I'm never lettin' you go, Smokeshow. That's my truth and it always will be." He presses me back down into the bed and starts to kiss me again in all the right places, his big body enveloping mine as if any space between us is too much.

"Round two?" I ask, just as Ty's stomach rumbles. "Or maybe we should order you some food?"

The question is answered as he rolls onto me fully hard and ready to show me again precisely what he needs right now.

It's not food.

His tongue worshipping, and his fingers strumming, all over me and into my most sensitive places, I lose my capacity for speech.

However, in this moment together with him I am consumed by my own important truth.

I love this beautiful hockey boy with all my heart.

How glad I am that I walked outside that tattoo parlor door months ago simply to offer a listening ear.

Because, it doesn't matter how our worlds intersected, how I thought I'd feel smothered if I loved a hockey boy. Turns out, we are the best fit because I understand him. The pressure. The ferocity. The strength. The devotion. After all, I've grown up with that for all my life.

I now know that all those qualities—which he throws passionately into hockey—will be how he passionately loves me with his whole brave and valiant heart.

Forever.

epilogue

Tyler

Two years and five months later.
December 24th
Saint Petersburg, Russia

Christmas in Saint Petersburg is like a realm where *Beauty and the Beast* met *Frozen* and had quintuplets. Old world architecture and golden palaces and churches covered in sparkling blue-white snow. Light parades and Christmas markets, endless holiday treats and decorations—all very fuckin' impressive for a kid all the way from South Boston who grew up with slim to none in the way of Christmas spirit.

But that changed after my first trip over here with Zo. My Christmas spirit is fuckin' overflowing now and I love coming to celebrate the holidays with my Russian smokeshow and her family. We're fully enjoying our third Christmas together, but I can say with certainty that it will not be our last.

This year we have a whole Crush gang at her parent's place celebrating Christmas Eve together. Boris and Talia have come today with Boris's mom who lives here. Irina, with her university professor man-bun-wearing *partner*, Oskar. Georg, Pam, Haley and Logan, of course. Even Vik and Scarlett and their two boys have joined the party along with Vik's mom who also lives in Saint Petersburg.

Right now, we're all at the Ice Palace skating in the middle of the city. Literally. As in...we're all ice-skating in front of a legit royal palace. The Winter Palace, home of the Russian czars. With the lighted trees, festive ice sculptures, and horse-drawn sleighs, it's like a really fancy North Pole village.

And the setting is pure perfection for what I'm about to do.

I'm skating with my girl, who looks like a goddess (as usual) in a long white sweater over her mile-long legs covered in warm leggings, with a matching scarf and hat and gloves in pale pink. She's my ice princess today, but only in the way of it being icy cold outside. Nothing about my Zo is icy. She's warm and loving and generous, and banging *hot* of course. Sexy as sin on skates. The first time we came here and did this I was blown-the-fuck-away. Not only by how gracefully elegant of a skater she is, but how sexy she looked skating in front of me. Most definitely a holy public erection, Batman! moment. I've had a lotta those moments since I found her, so I'm kinda gettin' used to them by now.

I signal to Pam and Georg to get the kids ready to

do their job. I can read Haley's lips as she asks Pam excitedly, "Is it time, Mommy?" Just watching their simple exchange fills my heart right up all the way to the top. The circle is closed now, and all is as it should be.

Their new birth certificates finally arrived a few months ago. My sister and brother are now Haley and Logan Kolochev, with a mother and father who love them like they should've been loved from the moment they were born. Their room at my place still gets plenty of use though, with a sleepover at least once a month. Georg and I are having an absolute blast coaching youth hockey with Evan and a few of our Crush teammates. Lots of players' kids are on the teams. Haley tried it but decided she liked figure skating better, so Mommy Pam has that firmly in hand. My little sis has some serious skills for only eight years old. Olympics, here we come.

Logan, on the other hand is all about the hockey. A freaking madman on skates at six. He's a natural, and I can't wait 'til the NHL draft comes around in about thirteen years. With his dad and his grandpapa and me of course, coaching him, the sky's the limit for the little pucker.

My ma chose to sever her rights—not for the benefit of her daughter or her son—but for money. I don't even know the amount, nor do I *ever* want to know. It's sealed away and doesn't change the outcome, which I *know* was only for the better. In the end, Georg and Pam were willing to negotiate a deal that my ma agreed to and signed off on. She relinquished her parental rights for cash. When she was released from jail and had access to her money, she up and disappeared. I haven't heard from her in nearly two years. No idea where she went or what kind of life she's living, or if she's even still with us. I can only wish for her to have found some measure of peace within her very broken soul—*namaste*. Beyond that, I've had to let her go for my own sake. Zen has been a life changer for me in so many ways.

I'm not alone anymore.

I have a family.

Who love *me*.

And I love 'em hard right back.

Zoya's mom, Marianna, full-on adopted me right from the first. She's like the coolest, most chill woman I've ever met. She's got nothing but hugs and kindness and love in her heart for her children and grandchildren. She was a schoolteacher before her recent retirement, so she's taken on the task of teaching me Russian. I'm gettin' there, but it might be a few more years 'till I'm able to pull it off in conversation with any skill. My understanding is decent, though. Got all the swears down first. Trash-talking is even more fun than it used to be behind the bench or in the box. There's a guy on Twitter who made an account just for my chirps. @KingORussiaChirpfest. My game chirps—wicked-clever Russian insults—translated for all to enjoy. Off-the-fuckin'-chain funny.

Zo's dad has been the biggest surprise of all. I thought he couldn't stand the sight of me, was merely tolerating my presence because he loves his daughter, but I was wrong.

When Dad's Week rolled around, I was prepared to go it alone, like I've done every other Dad's Week in all the years I've played hockey. It's a fun time where players' fathers or grandfathers or uncles join them for a whole week of games, usually one at home and two on the road. Dads fly with the team and have access to locker-room talks and every practice and game. Field trips, dinners, events happening throughout the week so there's media covering all the feel-good stories focusing on the families and their hockey lives.

So, the first Dad's Week since I found my Zo comes, and Kirill's there being interviewed with the other fathers. He tells them he's there to support "his three sons" on the Crush team. Georg, Boris, and ding-ding-da-ding…Tyler. Boris's father has never been in the picture, so Kirill stepped in when he was just a kid and put him in hockey, coached him. So, he's telling the interviewer about coaching the boys in youth hockey, watching them grow up and join the NHL, etc., and then he comes to me. He explains he was given a third son recently by his daughter, and that he is the proudest of *me,* not for the finely skilled defensive player I've become on the ice, but *the man I've become* off the ice. He calls me his *blagorodnyy syn.* Honorable son.

Whoa.

Coulda pushed me over with a feather during that interview. The look on my face, was complete and utter shock…and a whole lotta choked up, I gotta admit. Zoya watches the video all the time. She says she loves seeing my reaction, how my face changes when I understand what he's just said about me. And now, knowing what it's like to *receive* that unmistakable affirmation and love, it helps me love Zoya more, and know that my young siblings will have an incredible life. *Unconditional love.* Something I never thought I'd deserve. Especially from a parent figure.

Which made the conversation I had with him earlier today a wee bit easier, of course, but I would've still done it even if he hadn't changed his feelings about me. Because I asked him for his daughter's hand in marriage. Yeah, I did. And he gave his full blessing, thank you baby Jesus and all the angels. He knows how much I love my Zo, my Russian smokeshow princess.

The ring Vik helped me pick out for her is burnin' a hole in my pocket, and if I don't get it outta my pocket and on her finger real soon, I'mma need some medical attention.

For real.

Proposals? Some insanely stressful shit right here. Upped my romance game during the last two and a half years, though. When we first met, Zoya told me what she wished for in a guy and I've never forgotten what she said:

"I need a prince charming. Someone who will romance me. He will want to know everything about

me. And buy me flowers. He will make me feel like love is a fairy tale made real."

I don't know about the prince part for me, but I'm certain that she's my princess so I do my damnedest to make her feel like one. Flowers every time I come home from a long road trip, and now my attempt at a fairy tale made real.

I steer us over to the prearranged area on the ice where there's nobody skating, holding her hand in mine, checking her out to see if she suspects anything. She doesn't appear to as she smiles up at me, her cheeks flushed pink from the cold air.

"Why did you take your gloves off, Ty? Your hands must be freezing." I have no answer that I can share with her or I'll blow the surprise, so I just lean over to kiss her instead. And also, because well, I can't help myself. Princess looks like she needs kissing to me.

And I need to feel her lips against mine to steady my nerves before I do this thing. She tastes just as luscious as she always does, her lips warm and soft pressed to mine. When I finally break the kiss and pull my lips away, I see that everyone is in their places.

Go time, Lockhardt.

She sees what Haley and Logan have made just as I take her hands in mine and go down onto one knee.

My little bro and sis have skated a giant heart around us onto the ice with brooms dipped in pink metallic ice paint. The rest of our family and friends are now lined up along the edge of the heart, each of them holding a bouquet of pale pink roses. Except for

Vik, 'cause his hands are full of little boys—a toddler in one and a newborn in the other. Scarlett's busy filming all this for me.

"Zoya." I take a deep breath and look into her eyes which are now shining with happy tears...and know it's gonna be okay. "Zo, I love you so much you're a part of me now...and I want—*I need*—to spend the rest of my life with my best friend by my side." Releasing her right hand, I pull the box outta my pocket, flicking it open with my thumb."

She lets out a little cry when she sees the ring. It's set in platinum and yellow gold with three heart shaped diamonds, the largest in the middle with smaller ones locking it at center.

Locked hearts.

"These diamonds are locked hearts. They're locked in place, just as my heart is locked to yours. It can't ever be unlocked because there is no key for that. It's a permanent situation, babe. So...Princess Locked-Heart, will you make your bestie the happiest man in the world and be my wife?"

She's really got the tears flowing now, her head nodding and her bottom lip trembling, saying the only word I ever needed to hear from her, three times just to be safe, "Yes...yes...yes."

"Well, then..." I tug the glove from her left hand and manage to slip the ring onto her finger. I stare at it for a second and then bring her hand up to my lips for a kiss. "I love you, Princess Lockhardt." I might have some tears of my own 'bout to bust outta my eyes, so I do a thing I'm really fuckin' good at in such situations.

I joke about it.

"How was that, Smokeshow? Romancey enough for ya?"

"Oh yes." She's nodding and crying and laughing all at the same time. "So much. You're really nailing it —the charming prince thing," she says in her sexy Russian accent that has the power to undo me with a single word, let alone the few that come next. "I love you, yesterday, today, and tomorrow, my prince. *My Prince Lockhardt.*"

Again, saying all that to me in her Russian accent? Off-the-charts banging hot.

Then she pulls me up and before I know it, she's in my arms...and I can twirl us around on the ice just like a Disney prince and princess at the end of the movie. Of course, I can't resist throwin' in a cheesy wink for Scarlett's camera.

This shit's gonna play so well on video.

AND THEN THEY LIVED HAPPILY EVER AFTER...

my thoughts about...

afterword

EXTENSIVE CREATIVE LICENSE WAS APPLIED IN portraying some elements of NHL games, fan events and awards, that would ***not happen in real life***. I did this intentionally to create a more enjoyable reading experience within the storyline. These stories have been carefully crafted for your reading pleasure and in no way meant to be a true and accurate representation of NHL best practices and/or official rules currently or in the past.

Hockey Romance F-I-C-T-I-O-N all the way!!!

vegas crush by trope

All books in the ***VEGAS CRUSH*** series are *STANDALONES* existing in a connected world centering around a Las Vegas ice-hockey team. You can read them out of order if you wish and everything will still make sense with only minor spoilers. I've made a list of tropes for you here.

CRUSHED

BOOK 1

Forbidden, Reformed "Player", Ukrainian/American Hero, Good Girl Heroine, Office Romance, Love in the Workplace, He Falls First, Sports Romance, Team Captain, Social Media Manager, Risking it All for Love, Band of Brothers

BOOK 2

Bad Boy Russian Hero, Virgin Heroine, Damaged Heroine, Forbidden, Office Romance, Hockey Defenseman, Team Physical Therapist, Love in the Workplace, Band of Brothers, Overcoming Self-Doubt and Addiction, Trust

RED ROCKET

BOOK 3

Grumpy/Sunshine, Russian Hero, Feisty Red-Haired Heroine, Forbidden, Office Romance, Hockey Defenseman, Public Relations Manager, Love in the Workplace, He Falls First, Brooding Alpha, Opposites Attract, Band of Brothers

PUCK MONEY

BOOK 4

Opposites Attract, Forbidden Romance, Financial Advisor/Client Relationship, Russian/Romanian Hero, Nerdy Young Heroine, Fresh Start in Vegas, Dyslexic Hero, Gentleman Alpha, Good Guy Hero, He Falls First, Age Gap, Vegas Mafia Suspense, Savior Hero, Band of Brothers, Superstar Hockey Centerman

BOOK 5

Friends to Lovers, Teammates Little Sister, Young Virgin Heroine, Russian Heroine, Boston Native, Bad Boy Hero, Forbidden Romance, First Love, Age Gap, Single "Dad" Vibes, Hardscrabble Upbringing, Band of Brothers, Hockey Defenseman, New Adulting, Found Family

BOOK 6

Enemies to Lovers, Forced Proximity, Love in the Workplace, Neuro-Diverse Hero, French-Canadian Hero, Rock Chick Heroine, Socially Awkward w/ No Filter, Opposites Attract, Instant Attraction, Fish Out of Water, Band of Brothers, Superstar Hockey Goalie, Rockstar Heroine, Brooding Alpha, Guitar Lessons w/ Cute Kids, Personal Growth, Sacrificing for Love

BOOK 7

Surprise Pregnancy, One Night Stand, Forbidden
Romance, Love in the Workplace, Boss/Employee,
Office Romance, Sneaky Dates, Instant Attraction, Age
Gap, Mature Hero, Gentleman Alpha, Love After
Divorce, Can't Keep Their Hands off Each Other, Career
Milestones, Team General Manager, Team Nutritionist

BOOK 8

Friends With Benefits, Instant Attraction, He Falls First,
Brooding Alpha, Superhero Complex, Gentleman Alpha,
Damsel in Distress, Knight in Shining Armor, Living up to
Father's Legacy, Vegas Mafia Suspense, Comic Book
Nerd, Wedding Planner Heroine, Band of Brothers,
Finding Your Voice, Parent/Child Relationships

BOOK 9

Age Gap, Secret Crush, Surprise Pregnancy, Shotgun Wedding, Opposites Attract, The Owner's Granddaughter, The Brooding Hockey Player, Forced Proximity, Only 1 Bed, Career Milestones, Forbidden, Old Family Friends, *Neanderthal* Hero, *Heiress* Heroine, Parenthood, Beliefs, Growing Up, Manning Up, Facing Your Demons, Family Legacy

BOOK 10

Christmas Marriage Proposal, No Third-Act Breakup, Proposal Problems, Brooding Hockey Player Hero, Buying a Home, Festive Holidays, Dear Santa Letter, Gentleman Alpha, Building a Legacy, Comic Book Nerd, Wedding Planner Heroine, Team Captain, Band of Brothers, Family Relationships, OTT Romantic Gifts

about the author

BRIT DEMILLE is the alter ego of *NYT* Bestselling author, Raine Miller, having an absolute blast writing books quite different from what she writes as Raine.

Stories about sexy billionaires [millionaires make the cut too] who fall in instalove with young women who may or may not be virgins, and then go on to make adorable babies together are her favorite themes. In addition to the billionaires, hot hockey players are at the top of her list of favorite heroes, along with royals and ex-military bodyguards.

Most important when she writes a story is a happily ever after. But during the actual *writing* of the story, the most important thing is a cup of hot tea with a splash of milk (and don't forget the stash of cherry Jolly Ranchers). A dog or two will likely be in between her and the chair at any given moment, which is very handy, because they are the ones who approve everything she writes.

RAINE MILLER is a #2 *New York Times*, *USA Today*, and *Wall Street Journal* bestselling author since 2012. Before that, she spent two decades teaching kiddos to read—something she's most proud of. These days, writing steamy romance books pretty much fills up the hours...for which she keeps pinching herself to make absolutely sure she's not dreaming.

#Truth

She has a handsome husband, two amazing sons, and two very bouncy Italian greyhounds to keep her busy the rest of the time. Her boys know she writes romance books but gratefully they have zero interest in reading even a single one. *Thank. God.*

When she's not writing she's likely deep into a hockey game cheering on her beloved *VEGAS GOLDEN KNIGHTS* and dreaming up a new book. The greyhounds are likely to be in her lap while she writes the books or watches hockey—both dogs at the same time of course!

She loves to hear from readers and chat about the characters she's created.

You can connect with Raine on Facebook in her reader group, **Raine Miller Romance Readers.** She pops in to visit most days because it's a super happy place where romance awesomeness abounds day in and day out with the most amazing readers on earth.

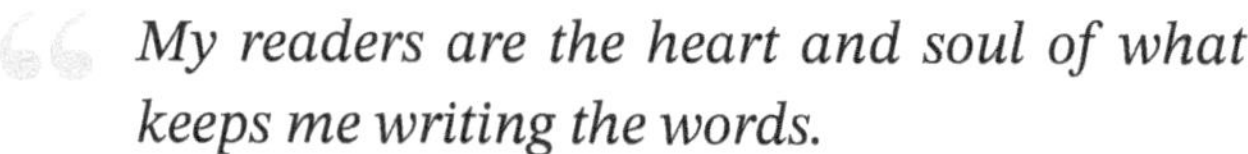

My readers are the heart and soul of what keeps me writing the words.

#Truth2

also by raine miller

The BLACKSTONE AFFAIR

NAKED, Part 1

ALL IN, Part 2

EYES WIDE OPEN, Part 3

RARE and PRECIOUS THINGS, Part 4

The ROTHVALE LEGACY

PRICELESS, I

MY LORD, II

BLACKSTONE DYNASTY

FILTHY RICH, I

FILTHY LIES, II

HOCKEY ROMANCE *as Brit DeMille*

CRUSHED, Vegas Crush #1

SIN SHOT, Vegas Crush #2

RED ROCKET, Vegas Crush #3

PUCK MONEY, Vegas Crush #4

SMOKESHOW, Vegas Crush #5

The KEEPER, Vegas Crush #6

LUCKY PUCK, Vegas Crush #7

Mr. HOCKEY, Vegas Crush #8

CLUSTERPUCK, Vegas Crush #9

Mr. HOCKEY's MARRY CHRISTMAS, Vegas Crush #10

CONTEMPORARY ROMANCE

CHERRY GIRL

HUSBAND MATERIAL

LOVELY PINK

HISTORICAL ROMANCE

The MUSE

The PASSION of DARIUS

The UNDOING of a LIBERTINE

Wedding Night Diaries

LORD BLACKWOOD'S VIRGIN

join raine mail

For my newsletter and information on upcoming books and events, you should definitely sign up for Raine Mail. Use the QR code below.

whispers *There's so many freebies in that thing.*

subscribe to Raine Mail